W9-CFO-892

MAYHEM IN THE MUDROOM

MOORECLIFF MANOR CAT COZY MYSTERY BOOK 5

LEIGHANN DOBBS

CHAPTER ONE

Araminta Moorecliff eyed her Siamese cats, Arun and Sasha, as they paced back and forth in the entryway to the dining room, their tails raised straight in the air. This did not bode well, she thought as she tracked the movements of the sleek creatures with their velvety brown-and-cream-colored fur. As she watched, they turned their intelligent sapphire eyes in her direction, causing a feeling of disruption deep in her gut. Or perhaps that was the little rounds of salami she'd just eaten from the charcuterie board.

The stiff pacing was the exact thing the cats did when they'd discovered a body. But that couldn't possibly be the case now; she'd just barely solved the murder that had plagued the Moorecliff annual cat show earlier that very day.

Now that the show was over and the murder solved, most of the guests and contestants were packing up to leave. Araminta was relaxing in the mansion's opulent

1

dining room with friends and family, including the newly freed murder suspect, one of her oldest friends, Daphne Burgess.

Daphne had been falsely accused of murdering another of the contestants, Nina Bellaforte. Luckily, Araminta had cleverly deduced the identity of the real killer, and Daphne had been released and was currently assuring everyone at the table that she'd had complete faith in Araminta all along.

"I knew Araminta would figure out who really killed Nina, but I never dreamed I might be awarded the grand prize for a contest in which I wasn't even permitted to compete!" Daphne sighed with contentedness as she popped a grape into her mouth.

Since Daphne had been arrested at the beginning of the competition, she'd been unable to compete. The cash prize had been won by Bjorn, the cat of Stephen Roy, whom Araminta now knew was the new leader of the local crime ring. Apparently, even some crime ring leaders had a good heart, because he'd given up the prize money to Daphne, stating that he already had plenty of money and winning was enough for him.

"That was very nice of him," Daisy, Araminta's niece-in-law, said. It was so like Daisy to think of a crime boss as "nice." She saw the best in everyone, and her generous nature wasn't the only thing Araminta liked about her. When Araminta's nephew, Archie, had died, Daisy had taken over the head-of-household duties at Moorecliff Manor. Some might have doubted if Daisy was up to the task, but not Araminta. She knew the vivacious blonde was more than just a pretty face.

"It was, but not so sure it warranted you inviting him to stay here," Stephanie, Araminta's grandniece, said. "I mean, he is a criminal, and Ivan is a detective. Might not be good for his career to be seen cavorting with Mr. Roy."

"Daisy was just being polite. I'm sure they won't be here long." Araminta was surprised Stephanie had taken her attention from Detective Ivan Hershey long enough to be aware of the conversation. The two of them had been making moon eyes at each other for months now, and while they thought they were being discreet, it was no secret to everyone else.

But Stephanie had a point. Araminta didn't love the idea of Stephen and his fiancée, Vivianne Underwood, staying at the manor either. At least they hadn't joined in their little snack tonight. Her eyes slid to the door, expecting Stephen and Vivianne to appear at any moment. They didn't... but the cats were still there.

"It seemed the least I could do," Daisy said cheerfully. "He was the winner, and the cat show did raise a lot for charity."

"Despite the murder," Ivan admitted. "Thanks again for your help, Araminta."

Araminta's cheeks heated. "Well, I couldn't have done it without your grandfather."

"Yes, where is Jacob?" Daphne frowned at the empty chair Jacob Hershey had occupied earlier in the evening.

3

The occupants of the table had dwindled over the past hour, and Jacob wasn't the only one missing. Bartholomew Belamie, or Bertie, as Araminta called him, had also been enjoying an evening of camaraderie with the group as another longtime friend of Araminta and Jacob. Each man had left the table within five minutes of the other, to be precise, which was odd to Araminta, especially after the way Jacob had been behaving over the past few days whenever Bertie was around.

Bertie's young assistant, Stella, had been at the table too, but she'd left shortly after Bertie and Jacob. Apparently, she knew one of the reporters who had attended the show, and she wanted to see him out.

A commotion in the hallway interrupted Araminta's thoughts.

They all glanced toward the door, and Daisy rose from her seat. "I'll go see what that is and make sure the rest of the stragglers find their way out."

Araminta's eyes were drawn to the cats again. When everyone had been at the table, the cats, along with Jacob's cat, Codger, had been resting in front of the fire. Now Codger was missing, and Arun and Sasha were doing their disturbing dance.

Her suspicions tweaked, Araminta waved to Moorecliff Manor's butler, Harold, and whispered for him to seek out Jacob—discreetly, of course—to make sure nothing untoward was going on between the two men. While Bertie had been his usual fun-loving self during the past few days, Jacob was more gruff than

4

usual whenever he was near, and he'd become more so every time he saw Bertie and Araminta together. She was worried there might be some secret feud going on between the two of them, but she could not begin to fathom what that might be. They were friends.

While she waited for Harold to return, she chatted with Ivan and Stephanie. Were the two of them holding hands under the table? It was hard for Araminta to tell.

Araminta glanced at her watch. At least a quarter hour had passed since she'd sent Harold to check on Jacob, and she was starting to get antsy. She didn't like the sinking feeling in the pit of her stomach. Just as Ivan was in the middle of recanting an old case—Stephanie appeared enthralled; Araminta thought it quite boring —Harold appeared, wearing a sober expression. He made his way to her side.

As soon as he neared her, he stopped, cleared his throat, and shuffled his feet until Araminta waved him closer. "Harold, is everything all right?"

Harold clasped his hands together and slowly turned his head from side to side. "There's been a bit of mayhem in the mudroom, Ms. Moorecliff. I'm afraid you will have to come see for yourself."

"Is Araminta getting slower at noticing our hints, or is it my imagination?" Arun asked as they looked down the hall. Araminta hadn't been the only one to follow

Harold, and they were now watching everyone who had been at the table hurry toward the mudroom.

"She doesn't seem to be catching on any quicker, but seeing as she just solved a murder, maybe we could cut her some slack," Sasha said.

"At least they're heading in the right direction." Arun turned his attention to the dining table. "And since they are all gone, maybe we could help ourselves to some of that delicious cheese."

Arun started toward the table, but Sasha interrupted him. "Wait! Trinity is cleaning up. She'll shoo us off the table before we can even get a bite."

Arun rolled his eyes. "Seriously? I bet we can jump up, run past, grab a morsel of cheddar, and be off the table before she even notices."

Sasha seemed reluctant. "I really don't want to be shoved off. Sometimes she isn't very gentle."

"Why? We are agile and fleet of foot. I've seen you jump onto the top of the refrigerator in one leap." Arun licked his lips, disappointment settling in as Trinity covered the tray of cheese with a sterling silver dome. Perhaps she'd leave the salami uncovered.

He glanced back at Sasha, who was still sitting in the doorway, now washing behind her left ear. "Is something amiss?"

"No. I just injured my paw a little. I don't want to make it worse by getting pushed off the table."

Arun had never known Sasha to back down from a challenge, but they were getting older, and injuries were bound to occur. Hopefully, nothing serious was wrong.

6

And anyway, she was looking a little heavy. Maybe it was better if she kept the snacking to a minimum, though he would never mention it to her. He'd made the mistake of mentioning her weight once before, and the comment had been met with an onslaught of hissing and clawing.

He decided to change the subject. "Hopefully, Codger is paying attention and can fill us in thoroughly. Perhaps we had better hurry to the scene of the crime."

"I'm sure Codger is watching everything and doesn't need us telling him what to do." Sasha seemed a bit put out on Codger's behalf. "And besides, Araminta is there and Ivan and Steph. Did you see Steph and Ivan holding hands under the table?"

"At least that's all they were doing," Arun joked.

Sasha sighed. "I've seen them taking lazy walks in the garden and kissing under the tree."

"Yech!" Arun turned away from the food on the table, his appetite ruined.

Sasha cleared her throat. "Yes, well, I think Ms. Steph is expecting a certain proposal."

"No! Surely they have not been together long enough for that?" Arun preferred long romances and not mushy ones either.

"When you know someone is right, you just know," Sasha said.

"I will never understand humans."

Arun glanced at Sasha. Cats did not have the same romantic fantasies—at least *he* didn't, though he was fond of Sasha, and they'd been together almost their whole lives. He couldn't imagine being with any other cat. In fact, he had to admit he was a little put out that Codger had nosed in on their partnership.

"We should go to the mudroom. I can understand why Araminta wouldn't catch on to our usual signal," Sasha said. "It's hard to believe another body could be at the manor so soon."

"Indeed, she will believe that soon enough."

"Unfortunately, this time the body is someone much closer to home."

CHAPTER TWO

Perhaps sensing this might be a police matter, Ivan had rushed ahead with Harold. Araminta had never seen Harold move so fast. The sinking feeling in her stomach became a twisty knot as they approached the mudroom, and Ivan rushed back out, holding up a hand to stop Stephanie from entering. "I think it's best you don't go in there, honey."

Honey? Araminta was curious about the public use of endearment but even more curious about what was in the room that he didn't want her to see. By the expression on Ivan's face, Araminta's worst fears had come true.

"Why not?" Stephanie craned to look over his shoulder into the room.

"Perhaps you could escort Daphne back to the dining room," Araminta suggested to her grandniece while shooting a look at Daphne.

9

Daphne caught on right away. "Oh dear me, has something horrible happened in there?" She flung the back of her hand up to her forehead. "My delicate senses…"

Araminta thought Daphne might be laying it on a bit thick, but her act did the trick. Stephanie swiveled her attention from the mudroom and took Daphne's elbow. "Let's just go back to the dining room."

"Thank you, dear." Daphne winked at Araminta behind Stephanie's back as the girl led her away. "I think a nice stiff whiskey might be in order."

Once Stephanie and Daphne were gone, Araminta steeled herself and entered the room.

There had been a struggle. The mudroom was seldom used for its true purpose these days. It had long ago become more of a storage room than a true route into the manor from outside, and there were various pieces of old furniture, art, and unused stools, cases, and such scattered around the room. An old brown wing chair had been pushed into the corner farthest from the door, and a green-and-gold-trimmed last-century commode sat near it on one side, an old sewing machine case on the other.

As she surveyed the room, ice filled the twisty, sinking pit in her gut. The door on the opposite side of the room that lead onto the paved stone walkway outside stood open, letting the cool evening air flood in.

Jacob was standing beside the door, an old ivory handled umbrella in his hand, his expression sour. He said nothing. He chose instead to wait in silence while Araminta surveyed the dastardly scene before her.

Reggie Moorecliff, Araminta's grandnephew, stood in the doorway, his expression grim. "Hello, Aunt Minta. I don't know what happened here. I had only just arrived. Harold asked me to wait here with Jacob until he could fetch you and Ivan to the... to the scene of the crime."

Araminta nodded but said nothing. Out of the corner of her eye, she noticed Bertie's royal-purple ribbon-trimmed fedora. It hung off one of the wings that made up the side of the wing chair.

A case of very expensive jewelry sat open on the chair's seat. A jeweler's display, which should have been sitting upright on the sewing machine case, had fallen on its side. The string of pearls it was supposed to demonstrate hung off it at an odd angle. An old wooden footstool had been carelessly pushed to one side, away from the chair, and Bertie... Bertie was lying on the floor behind it.

The ice in Araminta's stomach turned into a fist as she looked down at him. His eyes were open, his face twisted in a grimace, his throat a large purple bruise with a small bloody hole in the middle.

Bertie was dead, and that was horrible, but that wasn't the worst part. Judging by the size of the hole and the tip of the umbrella, the worst part was that Jacob appeared to be holding the murder weapon.

ARAMINTA TURNED to pin Jacob with a stare of inquisition. "What on earth happened here, Jacob?"

Between the ice now starting to chill her veins and the pain of suspicion growing deep in her heart, there was no way to control the unusual quiver present in her tone. She did not want the thought to manifest, and yet, somehow, it did...

Had Jacob killed their longtime friend?

Jacob turned to look at her, then his gaze shuttered. "He is dead, Araminta."

Of course Jacob had had nothing to do with it. But with what she'd seen here and after the way he'd acted the past few days and how tense things had been between him and Bertie and the umbrella with the bloody tip in his hand...

"I can see that, Jacob! In fact, we all can! But you haven't answered my question. What *happened?*" She nodded toward the umbrella, and Jacob jumped as if startled.

He glanced down at the umbrella then up at Araminta. "I didn't kill him, if that's what you think."

Araminta glanced at Ivan. He seemed completely perplexed. His grandfather—his gruff, blustery, sweet, and loving grandfather whom he would not be allowed to help this time—stood blithely between that body and an open door through which he could have easily escaped, insisting he hadn't killed the man at his feet, though clearly he was holding the item that had sent Bertie to his death.

Ivan sighed. "I have to call this in. They will send in

another detective to investigate, of course. After four murders here, I am certain you all know the procedure…"

"Meow!" Codger, Jacob's fluffy black-and-gray cat who had been sitting silently at Jacob's feet, made it clear he took a dim view of Ivan calling it in.

Araminta felt the same. She knew he would have to report the death eventually, but a few moments of delay would allow her to assess the scene and clues before the police shooed her away. "Wait. Just a few minutes, please, Ivan."

Ivan glanced from Araminta to Jacob, clearly rattled. "I'm sorry, Araminta. And I'm sorry for you, too, Grandfather, but this is my job."

"Wait!" Araminta demanded again, and Ivan paused for a moment to look over his shoulder at her with a pained apology in his eyes. Araminta strode to the open door. "You'll get better reception out there."

"Don't touch anything," Ivan warned as he slipped out the door

Araminta turned back to stare up at Jacob. "In the meantime, Harold, please fetch Daisy. Jacob, dear, you have to tell us everything you know—and be quick about it. We don't have much time to figure out what happened."

"Bertie was laying on the ground when I got here, Araminta. He had this"—Jacob lifted the umbrella— "sticking out of his throat. I tried to pull it out, thought I could save him, but he was already gone."

"But *what* were you doing here?" Araminta asked.

13

Jacob sighed. "After he left us at dinner, I came here to—well, the why doesn't matter, really. When I opened the door, I saw him laying there and hurried to his side. But I was too late."

His brief explanation given, Jacob stopped Ivan as he came back in the door and handed him his wristwatch then gestured toward Bertie. "I stopped it at the precise moment I was sure he was no longer with us."

Ivan looked at the time. *7:23 p.m.* Looking up at his grandfather with pride for using such an old-school tactic, he nodded. "Thank you. It would be a bit difficult to be more precise than this without—"

His breath caught, and Jacob patted his shoulder.

"You've done your job, boy, and I'm proud of that. You shouldn't give special favors to me, even if I am your grandfather."

"Who will they send in your stead, Ivan?" Araminta asked. "I don't think I can trust…"

Daisy walked into the room with Harold right behind her. "Reggie! You're home!"

He nodded, but when he didn't move forward to give her a hug hello, Daisy glanced around the room. Her gaze fell on Bertie. "Oh dear, not again. What's happened, Araminta?"

"I'll explain later," she told Daisy then gestured for Ivan to continue.

"I'll recommend the best, Araminta. You won't have to worry. I'd never leave my grandfather in just anyone's hands. You have my word."

Araminta turned to Jacob, her expression earnest.

"Who did you pass on the way here? When did Reggie arrive? Was there anyone else in the room?"

Jacob shook his head. "There was no one here. Reggie arrived right after I stopped my wristwatch—less than two minutes after. Harold came about the same time."

"I saw Mr. Belamie on the floor, with Mr. Hershey leaning over him. He looked at me and said, 'He's dead.' And that's when I asked Master Reggie to stay with him while I fetched the rest of you," Harold told her.

"What about Stella? She left the dinner table shortly after you did." Araminta was grasping at straws, but what if Stella's story about seeing the reporter out was a lie?

"I saw her before I came here, but she wasn't near the mudroom at all. She was in the front parlor."

"She could have been here before you. She could have killed Bertie!" Araminta declared, but Jacob shook his head no.

"She would never kill him, Araminta. He gave her a chance when she needed it, and she has always been grateful to him for that. Nothing could make her repay him in such a horrific fashion."

Araminta didn't like what he was saying at all. For Jacob to be the only possible suspect was appalling. But there had been other people in the mansion at the time —the stragglers who hadn't left. Any of them could have done it.

"Did you see anything, Reggie? Anyone running out as you came in?"

Reggie shook his head and looked down at Codger. "Just this guy here. He was running back from out in the garden."

Codger let out a mournful meow, and Jacob bent down to pet him. "Sorry, old boy, we might not get to go home just yet." Jacob glanced up at Araminta, his eyes moist. "If anything happens, will you take care of him?"

"Yes, of course." Araminta looked down at Codger, who was swishing his tail back and forth, staring at her with intelligent golden eyes. Had he been chasing the killer? If only cats could talk. Araminta felt that she would have solved quite a few cases a lot faster with the input of Arun and Sasha.

Speaking of which… The two cats had joined them and were prancing around Jacob's feet.

Araminta turned to Daisy. "What about that ruckus in the hallway? Could it have been the killer?"

Daisy pressed her lips together. "I don't think the timing is quite right. That was Dr. Perkins and his wife, Maisie. She hit a plant stand with her walker, toppled a vase full of gladiolas. They were the last ones out."

Araminta's suspicions flared. The Perkinses were clients of Bertie's. In fact, Maisie had several pieces from him. But no, she really was just grasping. The timing wasn't right at all if they'd been in the hallway when the crash happened, and Maisie could hardly move quickly with that walker.

She asked Harold to give an immediate and accurate accounting of every person within the manor at the time of Bertie's death, but it was not helpful at all. With the exception of Bertie's assistant, the reporter who had been on his way out the door, and Mr. and Mrs. Perkins, everyone else had already gone.

"Vivianne is still here," Daisy said. "Stephen too. Trinity mentioned earlier in the day that Vivianne wanted to speak with me before they left the manor about using the gazebo near the willows by the lake for her and Stephen's wedding venue. They will be leaving tomorrow."

"A wedding? At Moorecliff?" Harold brightened at the prospect then, recalling the severity of the moment, hurriedly schooled his features into something more sober. "My apologies, madame."

Daisy gave him a slight smile. "It's quite all right, Harold. With all the mischief and mayhem we've been dealt these past months, no one faults you for being excited over the prospect of happier times."

"Stephen Roy! He's the new crime boss!" Araminta looked at Jacob again. "He may have been innocent where Nina was concerned, but what about Bertie?"

Jacob shrugged. "Knowing what you know about him, he would be an easy suspect to accuse. Did anyone see him with or watching Bertie during the competition?"

The collective answer was no.

Glancing downward, Araminta felt tears prick her eyelids. Bertie—dear, sweet, fun-loving Bertie—was

17

gone, and if she didn't come up with some viable suspects right away, then Jacob might go to jail as his killer.

CHAPTER THREE

Araminta surveyed the crime scene while her mind raced to compile a list of suspects.

Who had still been in the mansion at the time of Bertie's death? There had been some stragglers from the cat show and, of course, everyone who had been around the dining room table. Daisy, Stephanie, and Ivan were in the clear; they had been with Araminta. But what about Stella and the reporter? Stephen Roy and Vivianne had been somewhere in the mansion too.

What had Bertie been doing in the mudroom? His jewelry display cases were out, which seemed to indicate someone wanted to peruse his stock. Daisy had said Stephen Roy and Vivianne were engaged. Maybe they had been looking for a ring? An engagement ring from Bertie was very desirable.

But if that were the case, why was Jacob here?

Arun and Sasha had trotted in and were weaving through the legs of the wing chair, their tails jerking in

19

the air as they meowed softly. Arun, careful not to disturb anything, sniffed the jewelry case.

Araminta stared at the case. "This obviously had something to do with the jewelry, but what? And why harm Bertie over it?"

Araminta's thoughts went to Jacob again. He'd never said anything outright, but Araminta got the feeling he hadn't liked that Bertie had become a wealthy, renowned jeweler. Every time it was mentioned, he turned gruff and changed the subject… unless Araminta shushed his objections and asked Bertie to continue. Bertie always had adventurous stories to share, all related to his now-famous jewelry business. Hadn't she done so more than once during the past three days?

Her gaze went back to Jacob, and her lungs squeezed tightly in her chest, practically stifling her. Fighting the discomfort, she straightened her back and drew in a deep, calming breath, forcing the air in and out again while denying the worrisome whispers in her head. Of course Jacob could not have done this. The very idea was preposterous.

Jacob was innocent. He had to be. She would find Bertie's killer. She would clear Jacob's name and see him freed. Above all, she would prevail. In this case, she had to, because the alternative—living out the rest of her years without Jacob Hershey in her life—was suddenly utterly unthinkable.

Her resolve firmly in place, Araminta walked to Daisy and whispered, "Do you have your phone?"

Daisy nodded. "I do."

"Take pictures of everything but touch nothing. Get at least three angles of all that you see, and do hurry. If I know Ivan, the police will be arriving soon."

"Araminta," Jacob called to her, dragging her attention away from the crime scene.

Steeling herself against the soothing tone in his voice, Araminta said, "Can it wait, Jacob? There are clues we need to catalog before they're removed, in order to save your wretched skin. Unless you see something I don't…"

Holding out his hand to her, he shook his head. When her fingers touched his, he pulled her close and stared into her eyes. "Araminta, I am so sorry. About Bertie, I mean. I know what he meant to you."

Araminta's eyes misted. She shook her head and pulled away. "There's no time for that, Jacob, and no need to be sorry. You're innocent and have nothing to apologize for."

"Is there anything I can do—before the others get here?" he asked her, his expression both grave and sincere.

"Yes," she told him. "You can start thinking of all the many different ways to say 'I told you so' to Ivan's men once I prove to them that you are innocent."

UNFORTUNATELY, things didn't work out the way Ivan had planned. The station put Detective Harry

21

Bixcombe, instead of someone who would keep Ivan in the loop, in charge. Bixcombe was the most obnoxiously annoying detective in the precinct, and there was no love lost between him and Ivan. Detective Bixcombe appeared intent on arresting Jacob on the spot.

"We can't play favorites just because he's your grandfather." Bixcombe switched the toothpick from one side of his mouth to the other as he pulled out the cuffs and headed toward Jacob.

"But we haven't even investigated!" Ivan said.

Bixcombe leveled a look at him with his beady black eyes. "He was holding the murder weapon."

"He had pulled it out of his neck, trying to save the man," Araminta pointed out.

Bixcombe simply quirked a brow and slapped on the cuffs.

Everyone gave statements to the police. Daisy gave the investigator details for the reporter who had been in the manor but on his way out within the time frame in which Bertie's death had occurred. The medical examiner took Bertie's body away, and the police taped off the entrances to the mudroom, as it was now a crime scene.

Apparently, all these goings-on were too much for Vivianne and Stephen Roy. They'd packed up their bags and left in a hurry after giving a statement to the police. Araminta happened to overhear them tell Bixcombe that Vivianne had been suffering from a terrible headache and had been resting in the room since dinner. Stephen claimed to have been with her the whole time, each providing the other with a convenient alibi. When they'd heard about the murder, they'd decided not to stay at the manor. Even the town's biggest crime lord didn't want to stay in a home where there had been yet another murder.

After a long interrogation by police, Reggie trundled off to his rooms, promising to catch up with his family in the morning, but Bertie's assistant, Stella, bless her, was beside herself with shock and grief. With Bertie gone, she hadn't a clue what to do.

"Poor Bart! I simply must take care of his things and call his family." Stella sniffed. Like most everyone but Araminta, she'd called him Bart. Bertie was a special name only Araminta used for her old friend. "He only has one elderly sister left, and she's in a nursing home."

Daisy slid her arm around Stella's shoulders. "Now don't you worry. You can stay on here as long as it takes to get things sorted."

"Thank you, ma'am." Stella let Daisy lead her away toward her room.

For Araminta, watching the local police lead Jacob away in cuffs was one of the hardest things she had ever had to do. Assuring Ivan that his elderly grandfather would be fine in a jail cell downtown while she and the others figured out what really happened to Bertie was another.

"I really wish I didn't have to recuse myself from this case," Ivan said to Araminta as he watched the

23

police lead his grandfather away. "Who better than I to clear Grandfather?"

Araminta placed a hand on his arm. "Don't you worry. We'll get him cleared. It shouldn't take long if we put our heads together. Will you keep tabs on what's happening down at the police station?"

Normally, Ivan would never divulge the specifics of an ongoing case, but this one was different. They were on the same side, and with that sort of insider information, closing the case should be easy peasy. If Detective Bixcombe actually gave Ivan information, that was.

Ivan looked doubtful at first but then must have realized it was the best way to help Jacob. "I suppose I can in this case. Since I'm not officially on it."

"Good boy. Now why don't you go say goodbye to Stephanie. I think I will retire to my rooms and let my subconscious work on solving this crime."

"I DON'T NEED your human to coddle me," Codger said later that night as he smoothed the fur that Araminta had ruffled while petting and soothing him.

Arun glanced over. "Seems like you enjoyed it to me."

"Ach! I was just making her feel needed. You see how upset she is."

"The poor dear." Sasha seemed on the verge of tears. "She really loved Bertie and cares a lot about Jacob."

It was a little past midnight, and the cats were roaming the halls of Moorecliff Manor. Typically, their nocturnal ramblings consisted of peeking into the nooks and crannies, looking for mice and jumping up on the various tables, challenging each other not to knock something off. But tonight was different, Arun had discovered something, and he wanted to show the others.

Arun cleared his throat and started to trot toward his destination. "Tell us again what you saw, Codger."

"When I arrived in the room, Bertie was already on the floor, and Jacob was trying to help him. The door to the outside was open, and I ran out, sensing the perpetrator had just exited."

"But you didn't see who it was?" Arun asked.

Codger grimaced. "Unfortunately, I did not. I only caught a glimpse of a shadow as they ran around the corner. But the scent was rather feminine."

"It was a woman?" Sasha asked.

"Indeed, I do believe it was."

"Well, at least that narrows it down. I just wish we could tell the police," Sasha said. "I do not think that Bixcombe is going to be very good for Jacob's defense. He seems eager to pin this on him. The other cops don't like Bixcombe much. I heard them talking, and they also believe Jacob to be innocent."

"Ivan seemed a bit upset to have Bixcombe in charge, but if Jacob is innocent, it will be proven so," Arun said.

Codger hissed. "He *is* innocent!"

"Calm down. I didn't mean to insinuate that he wasn't." Arun stopped in front of one of the guest rooms and pushed the door open with his paw. "And I think this room might hold a clue that will help us prove it."

Codger hissed again. "Isn't this the room that snotty Norwegian forest cat was in?"

Bjorn, the Norwegian forest cat who belonged to Stephen Roy, *was* a little stuck-up. Arun had tried to engage him in conversation, but he'd given terse one-word answers. As near as Arun could tell, Bjorn preferred to stay in his crate, lie on his silk pillow, and eat sardines.

Arun sniffed the air. "He *is* snotty, and I can still smell those sardines they were feeding him. Yech."

"I don't know. He's rather a pretty cat." Sasha took a few seconds to preen then glanced up to see the others staring at her "What? He did win the cat show."

Codger snorted. "I suppose. But he wouldn't have won if the show was based on personality."

"Forget about him. Check this out." Arun trotted over to the bed and lifted the bed skirt.

Sasha and Codger poked their heads under. After a few seconds, Sasha backed out and looked quizzically at Arun. "A camera?"

"It must be Vivianne's. She was taking pictures everywhere," Codger said.

Arun sat up straighter. "Yes, she seemed to favor taking them of *me*. There was one on the stone wall in the garden and another on the stairs and—"

Codger cleared his throat. "Yes, well, what you make of this camera? Why do you think it was under the bed?"

"It must have fallen under. They got out of here pretty quickly, and from what I've seen in this room, they weren't the neatest of people," Arun said.

Sasha nodded. "I overheard that Vivianne is a little absent-minded. She had several cameras, and if one fell under the bed, she might not notice."

"Do you think this camera holds a clue?" Codger asked.

Arun shrugged. "Maybe. Maybe not. But I know one thing—we need to get Araminta to discover it. If there *is* a clue on there, it could be the one thing that proves our case."

CHAPTER FOUR

The next morning, Ivan woke Araminta with a phone call. The cause of death was a blow to the windpipe. No surprise at that, but the part that was a surprise was that the killer had either gotten lucky, or they'd known exactly where to hit Bertie to cause almost immediate death.

"You probably noticed there wasn't a lot of blood," Ivan said. "The laceration from the sharp end of the umbrella didn't do him in. It was the fact that some of the small bones in the throat were broken, causing asphyxiation."

"What kind of knowledge would one have to possess for that?" Araminta herself had no idea where the exact spot was.

"Anyone with medical knowledge or someone who had been in the military or armed forces and knew defense training."

29

Araminta's stomach sank. "Like Jacob."

"Yes." Ivan took a breath. "But lots of other people have that knowledge. Do you know of anyone with that sort of training who was at the manor at that time?"

"I'll have to get back to you on that."

"Sorry I can't give you more information. Bixcombe isn't keen on telling me much, so I'm out of the loop. Luckily, no one around here likes him, so some of the other guys have been feeding me information."

"Well, at least there's that. Thanks for filling me in."

Araminta hung up. If she couldn't get good information from Ivan, that might hamper her efforts. She'd better hurry.

Now who would know exactly where to hit Bertie in the neck in order to kill him? Or maybe the assailant didn't actually mean to kill? Stephen Roy might have such knowledge—it seemed like someone in his line of business would want to have all sorts of defense training. Vivianne had told the police they were both in their room when the murder happened, but that wouldn't be the first time a woman had lied for her fiancé. Of course she wanted someone not in the family to be the killer, but Harold, Reggie, and Jacob had been right in the room, and she must look at them as suspects too.

Reggie had no such knowledge as far as Araminta knew, but Harold had served in the military when he was young.

Perhaps there would have been time for Harold to... But why would Harold wish Bertie harm? And if he wasn't the guilty party but had been there, if he'd known what happened, why would he cover for Jacob? Or perhaps Harold had done the deed, and Jacob... Would the two men cover for each other? Or for Reggie?

Araminta didn't like the direction her thoughts were heading, and she'd not even managed to dress yet! She scooped up Sasha and made her way to the wardrobe to choose her outfit for the day.

"I think something in magenta should do," she crooned to the cat before placing her down on the floor so she could pull out a magenta blouse and lime-green scarf. Arun trotted in and batted at the fringe on the end of the scarf.

"Now that I think of it, I believe Harold was in the dining room when the murder occurred. I didn't check my watch, but the timing doesn't fit for him to be the killer," she said to the cats. "I cannot account for Reggie personally, but I intend to speak with him first thing this morning."

"Meow!" Sasha seemed to take offense at her insinuation that Harold or Reggie could be responsible for what happened to Bertie.

"Oh, I know neither of them did it. I don't think Reggie even has the specialized knowledge. Though it is odd that he was sneaking in the back door..."

"Merow!" Sasha shook her head.

"Yes, of course I am sure he had a good reason. But I am also sure Jacob didn't do it."

31

"Meyowl!" Arun batted at a pair of shoes.

"What is it? Do you agree? Maybe you saw something?" Araminta frowned at the cat, who suddenly and randomly darted into the bedroom and under the bed.

"Hmmm, under the bed. I will keep that in mind." Araminta picked out the rest of her ensemble and proceeded to dress.

By the time she made it downstairs to the dining room for breakfast, the rest of the family were already there. Harold and Trinity were serving.

"If you don't mind, Ms. Daisy, I'd like to take the afternoon off. Vivianne is shopping for a wedding dress, and she invited me to come along," Araminta heard Trinity say.

"Good idea, Trinity. If you can keep Vivianne busy, that will give me plenty of time to speak with Mr. Roy about what happened here last night," Araminta announced as Reggie stood to help her with her chair. She murmured her thanks then asked how his visit to the West Coast division of the family business had gone.

"My trip went very well, Aunt Minta," he told her. "You'll be proud to learn I got a promotion."

After Archie's death, Reggie had taken an interest in the family business. Under Daisy's expert tutelage, it seemed he was doing well. Araminta was glad to see the boy had settled down and was taking things seriously.

"We should celebrate, Reggie," Daisy said, "but we will wait for a more appropriate time, of course."

Stephanie, Araminta noticed, was quiet. She sipped

at her tea far more than she nibbled at the food Trinity had placed in front of her.

Araminta dug into her scrambled eggs. "Ivan called. Jacob is doing well under the circumstances."

At the mention of Ivan, Stephanie brightened. "Did he sound upset, Aunt Minta?"

Araminta sipped her tea. "Of course he sounds upset—his beloved grandfather is in jail."

Stephanie seemed to deflate at her words, and Araminta felt bad, so she continued. "Ivan is doing his best to remain calm and to assist the police in any way he can. He's strong, Steph. He will be all right, and so will Jacob."

Stella, Bertie's assistant, came into the dining room. After a brief greeting to everyone, Harold led her to a chair. "The police took Bart's jewelry."

"Evidence," Araminta told her. "They will examine it for fingerprints and other clues. But did you happen to look at it? Did you notice if anything had been taken?"

"The police showed me pictures, but I honestly don't know." Stella tucked a strand of blond hair behind her ear, and Araminta noticed a luminescent pearl-and-diamond earring. "I do hope the jewelry will be returned after. There were some very important pieces on that tray. Well, important to Bart. I am sure he would not want anything to happen to them."

"Oh?" Araminta's sleuthing senses perked up. "Important in what way?"

Stella waved away her question. "Just that he chose them specifically for a special client." She stared at her plate, but her hands were fidgeting with the napkin she'd placed in her lap.

Araminta pressed on. "Who was the client? Was he here at the manor? Is that why Bertie brought jewelry along with him for his visit?"

Stella's cheeks turned red. "I—I really cannot say, Ms. Moorecliff. I've given my statement to the police, but Bart would not want me to say more. In deference to his memory, please, I would prefer if you did not press me on it further."

"Vivianne mentioned that she wanted an engagement ring from Belamie's," Daisy volunteered. "But to my knowledge, neither Vivianne nor Stephen had any dealings with Bart while they were here."

"He probably chose it from the shop in town, but I don't see how he could afford one," Stephanie said, her expression confused. "Belamie jewels are the best, and the most expensive in the world."

Araminta and Daisy exchanged a look, and Araminta nodded. She would need to speak with Ivan while she visited with Jacob this morning. If anyone would know the name Stella had revealed in her statement, it would be Ivan or one of his police friends. As for Stephen Roy being able to afford a ring from Belamie's, well… "There are things about Mr. Roy you do not yet know, Steph."

She couldn't say more. Not with Stella at the table. Later, she would fill Stephanie in about Stephen being the new crime boss, which meant he had access to more money than he could ever need in his lifetime. So if Stephen had killed Bertie, it most likely hadn't been to steal jewels from his display. So then what would his motive be?

CHAPTER FIVE

*A*fter breakfast, Araminta had the car brought around and headed into town. She needed to see Ivan, but first, she wanted to see Jacob. It took more than one call to arrange for visitation, but Ivan managed to pull it off. Unfortunately, Ivan seemed in the dark about any information Stella had given them. Was that because Bixcombe had kept the information to himself, or had Stella been lying about what she'd told the police? She had seemed rather evasive.

"Araminta, what are you doing here? Isn't there enough to keep you occupied at the manor?" Jacob asked as soon as he was led into the room where she waited.

"Of course there is plenty to keep me busy, but I need to speak with you, Jacob. About Bertie." She waited for him to get comfortable—as much as possible on the cold, hard chairs in the visitation area—then she asked, "Do you know who was buying jewelry from Bertie at Moorecliff?"

Jacob gave her a look. "Who mentioned that Bertie was selling jewelry at Moorecliff?"

"Why else would he have a display tray on hand? Stella told us the police took the jewelry as evidence, but she was concerned over a few special pieces Bertie had handpicked for someone."

"Who?"

"She wouldn't say, which is why I wanted to see you. I thought you might know."

"Bertie never mentioned anyone at the manor approaching him for jewelry to me," Jacob told her, but for some reason, Araminta thought he might not be telling the truth.

"Not even Stephen Roy?"

"Especially not Stephen. Bertie tends—tended to shy away from gentlemen of Mr. Roy's ilk. He runs a clean business, and dealing with a fellow of Roy's character might muddy the waters, if you catch my meaning."

She did. He was telling her that Bertie preferred not to do business with those who engaged in shady dealings, and she couldn't blame Bertie. "Stephen and Vivianne are recently engaged, and I thought perhaps Mr. Roy had commissioned something for her and met with Bertie at the manor. But if you say he did not, I believe you."

"Why do I sense hesitation in your tone?" Jacob asked.

"Because something isn't adding up. There were jewels at the manor, specific jewels if Stella is to be trusted and believed. If Bertie wasn't offering them, why bring them along?"

"I'm sure you will figure it out, Minta, but I must warn you not to go jumping to conclusions without investigating all the clues."

Araminta made a face. "Yes, Jacob. You've told me that many times before."

Jacob settled back in his seat. "Good, now can we speak of other things? How is Ivan? What has he said about the murder? How is Codger? I hope he's not giving you any trouble."

Araminta's heart softened at Jacob's look of concern for his cat. "Codger is fine. No trouble at all. Through I do sense he misses you." And then, since her allotted time for visitation was running out, Araminta quickly told him what Ivan had relayed on the phone about the cause of death and how Stephen Roy might have that knowledge. "I plan to speak with Mr. Roy while I am in town."

Jacob's brows drew together in a scowl. "Not alone, Araminta. You bring Ivan or your nephew, Reginald, along with you."

She waved away his concern. "Don't you worry about me, Jacob. I'll be fine. We are only going to have a chat, and I've already made the appointment, you see. Vivianne won't be there. She invited Trinity to shop with her today for a dress for her wedding."

"Wedding? I didn't realize that was happening so soon."

Araminta nodded just as the bailiff came to the door. "Daisy gave Vivianne and Mr. Roy permission to speak their vows at Moorecliff."

Jacob's gaze took on a faraway look. "I've always thought a wedding at Moorecliff would be a lovely affair."

"Really?" Araminta asked. "I never thought you contemplated such things as weddings."

He rose to follow the bailiff back to his cell. "There are a few things you don't know about me."

There was something in his tone when he spoke those cryptic words that set Araminta on edge. Had Jacob been keeping secrets from her? If he had, did those secrets involve Bertie? She tried to push the vague sense of foreboding from her thoughts as she left the precinct.

STEPHEN ROY MET Araminta in the lobby instead of having his temporary assistant escort her to his "office" in the back of the strip club where he did most of his business. "Ms. Moorecliff, how lovely to see you again. But you didn't need to make a trip down here just to thank me about the cat show."

Since Stephen's cat, Bjorn, had won the cat show and Stephen had been so kind as to give the money to Daphne, Araminta had used that as an excuse to make an appointment to speak to him. "It was a nice thing you did for Daphne, and I didn't get a chance to talk to you before you left the manor, with all the commotion and all. I felt it was important to thank you in person."

Stephen nodded. "It is nice of you to give your thanks in person. Much appreciated. I apologize that Viv is not here to see to your comfort. She had other priorities to see to today."

Araminta nodded. "The wedding dress, yes, I know. Trinity should be meeting her at Silver Linings as we speak."

He seemed surprised, then not. "The other Ms. Moorecliff mentioned the wedding?"

"She did. I'm sure you sent Viv with a bodyguard of some sort?"

Stephen's eyes narrowed, but his lips quirked in amusement. "Normally, I would protect her body... but today Chuck the chauffeur will be able to step in if there is trouble. We're all trained, you see. Are you worried about your maid's safety?"

"Oh, not really, just wondered if the girls would be able to engage in girl talk without someone looming around them."

Stephen laughed. "Don't worry. Chuck will keep his distance."

Araminta smiled. Stephen had just told Araminta what she needed to know. He was trained in defense. He was quickly becoming her top suspect. "Daisy also mentioned Vivianne wanted an engagement ring from Belamie's. Is that true, Mr. Roy?"

Stephen didn't hesitate. "Mr. Belamie has exquisite stock, yes. How could a man with such a treasure as Vivianne have anything else? Everyone who is anyone knows Belamie's fine jewels are the best—and I am definitely anyone."

"I see," Araminta said, but she didn't. Not really. Jacob had said that Bertie didn't want to sell a ring to Stephen, but Stephen made it seem like there was no problem. Perhaps Bertie had decided to sell to him after all? Or perhaps when Bertie refused to sell, Stephen had taken one by force.

The urge to ask to see a receipt was hard to resist, but she didn't want him to think she was accusing him of Bertie's murder. Not when she had nothing with which to back up the accusation. "Well, I suppose I shall be off. Thank you for your time, Mr. Roy. I am certain Miss Vivianne will treasure her engagement ring for the rest of her life, and she will be a beautiful bride."

"Thank you. With that, I agree most wholeheartedly, Ms. Moorecliff. I'm sure she will since she picked it out. I'm sorry for your recent loss, by and by. The world will certainly feel Mr. Belamie's absence."

"Indeed," Araminta agreed. She thanked him for his time again and made her way back to the car with more questions spinning in her head than had been there before her visit.

If Stephen had bought the ring from Belamie's, he would not have been the "special client" Stella mentioned, and he would have no reason to harm

Bertie. But if he wasn't the client Bertie was meeting at Moorecliff Manor, who was?

She had a sneaking suspicion Jacob knew more than he was saying, but she hadn't a clue why he was being so secretive about it. If he knew someone was buying jewels from Bertie at Moorecliff, why wouldn't he just say so? Especially if that person was a potential suspect who could help clear him of murder.

CHAPTER SIX

*B*ack home after her foray into town, Araminta waited in Daisy's office for Reginald. She'd sent Harold to ask him to join her the moment she'd arrived at the manor, but he hadn't yet put in the requested appearance.

A knock drew her attention. *Reggie, at last!*

Only it wasn't Reginald who came into the room. Stephanie hurried to the chair behind Daisy's desk and inserted a thumb drive into the computer. "These are the photos from Daisy's phone. She said you needed them as soon as possible, but I was thinking Ivan..."

Araminta was already clicking into the folders on the drive, looking at the photos. "Ivan's people have their own photographs. I asked Daisy to take these for me before the police arrived."

"Oh." Stephanie stepped back. "What are you looking for?"

45

"Anything that will point me in the direction of Bertie's killer," Araminta told her.

Another knock sounded, and Araminta minimized the screen. "Come in."

Reggie stepped into the room. "Harold said you wished to see me?"

"I do," Araminta told him. "I wanted to talk to you about last night, about when you arrived."

"Oh, of course." Smiling, he nodded at Stephanie. "Good afternoon, sis."

Araminta shooed Stephanie back around the desk but didn't ask her to leave. Stephanie sat beside her brother in a chair in front of the desk. Araminta knew what she was doing. She would listen in then report to Ivan. That was fine. The boy was worried silly about his grandfather, and there was little he could do to help solve the case.

"Tell me what you remember from last night, Reggie. From the moment the taxi dropped you off in the drive."

"Well…" He kicked back in the chair and propped one ankle over his knee. "Toledo Tom—that was the taxi driver's name. Or nickname. Whatever. He turned off the meter at seven-nineteen. I took my bag from the back. I remembered the annual cat show was wrapping up, so I came around to the mudroom. It's closer to my rooms, and I didn't want to disturb any last-minute cele- brations."

Stephanie straightened, though she'd been sitting stiffly on the edge of her chair. "Jacob stopped his

46

watch at seven twenty-three. It took you four minutes to walk around to the mudroom from the main drive?"

"Five," Reggie corrected. "When I came around the side of the house, I saw Codger on the side lawn, trotting back from the east end of the house. I stopped to give him a pet. The door to the mudroom was ajar, and when I opened it, I saw Jacob standing up from a crouching position. He was holding that cane and had put something in his pocket, which I now know was his watch. The other door opened, and Harold stepped inside. He took one look around then asked me to stay with Jacob until he returned with you."

"Did you see or hear anyone when you were going from the drive to the mudroom? Besides the cat."

"Not a soul. It was quiet too. Dark."

"Just the way you like it when you're trying to sneak in," Stephanie said. "Remember when we were going to that concert when we were in high school, and—"

"I wasn't sneaking. As I said, I remembered the contest and didn't want to intrude," Reggie said, cutting Stephanie off. He gave her a pointed look, and she grinned, but she didn't say anything else.

"Precisely," Araminta said. At least the timing definitely showed Reggie was not the killer. The meter on the taxi would prove that. Not that she had really suspected him. "And after Harold left the room to fetch me, what happened? Did Jacob say anything to you?"

"He said, 'Welcome home, boy. I hear you're doing what you can to make your father proud.' I said, 'Yes, sir.' He nodded, stuffed his hands into his pockets, and we waited in silence until you guys arrived."

"You didn't even bother to asked what happened?"

Reggie looked a bit discomfited. "If you will pardon my saying so, Aunt Minta, it was rather obvious what had happened."

"And what did you presume that to be, Reginald Moorecliff?" she asked him. How he answered would tell her a great deal about how he felt about Jacob.

"I saw Bartholomew on the floor and the pained expression on Jacob's face. I knew right away that something terrible had happened to the fellow, and Jacob wasn't too happy about either the fact it had happened or that he would now be forced to tell you. He knows how much you love Mr. Belamie, Aunt Minta."

Araminta felt relieved by Reggie's explanation. It meant he didn't believe Jacob was guilty of committing the crime himself and that Jacob's demeanor had not reflected guilt.

A third knock sounded on the office door, and this time, Harold poked his head inside. "Ms. Daisy asked me to let you three know lunch is ready when you're finished here."

"Oh, good!" Reggie stood. "I missed dinner last night and breakfast this morning, I'm afraid. Now, I'm feeling quite starved!"

Araminta's gaze sharpened on his face. "You should not miss meals, Reggie. It's bad for your health."

He nodded. "Which is precisely why I suggest you ladies allow me to escort you to the dining room."

"I WAS THINKING," Araminta said, addressing the group now seated at the Moorecliff dining table. "Who was that media fellow Stella was seeing off last night? Daisy, you are well acquainted with most of the employees from our local stations, are you not?"

Daisy spread her napkin in her lap and nodded. "Daryl Sendquist was the videographer streaming the live show. Do you think he had something to do with Bertie's death?"

"Murder," Araminta amended. "I'm not sure. Not really, but he would be the only one who did not give a statement to the police, as he was gone once they arrived. I would like to speak with him, if you could arrange it, Daisy."

"Of course. I'll put in a call after lunch," she promised.

Stella joined the family at the table shortly after, and Harold made the rounds, pouring lemonade from a glass pitcher into chilled glasses, which he placed beside each plate. Araminta waited until she was seated and had taken a refreshing sip from her drink before she asked, "Stella, how do you know Daryl Sendquist? Is he a friend?"

Her cheeks turned pink. She set her glass down and smoothed her napkin in her lap, just as Daisy had done earlier. "Family, actually, though few know of the connection."

Daisy leaned forward, a curious glint in her gaze.

"Family? I was not aware, and I know practically everyone down there. Is there a reason for keeping the connection out of general awareness?"

"Daryl didn't want special attention. People know I work for Bartholomew. He was quite a wealthy man, and I spent a great deal of time in his personal company. If people knew Daryl and I were related, they might think I had some arrangement with Bart, who might have pulled some strings with the higher-ups at the station to get Daryl hired."

"Of course that was not the case…" Araminta said, though she left the comment open.

"Absolutely not." Stella straightened in her seat. "My cousin, Daryl, is very good at his job. He was hired on merit alone."

"Were you accustomed to asking favors of Bertie?" Stephanie asked. She slanted a look at Daisy.

Stella's chin came up. "Are you accusing me of something, Miss Moorecliff?"

"No, I—" Stephanie started.

Stella was already on her feet, having tossed her napkin into her still-empty plate. "I appreciate the reason for your questioning—all of you," she said. "Bartholomew is gone, and we all are devastated. We want to know why, and we want justice for his death. But *I* am not a criminal."

She pushed her chair under the table, though she held on to the back of it with a white-knuckled grip while she visibly struggled to gain control of her emotions. "To answer your question, no. I never asked Bart for favors. He —he was good to me in a time when no one else was. After my nursing career was over, he gave me a job and a place to stay. But more importantly, Bart trusted me with his most valuable possessions, which should count for something."

She drew in another breath then continued. "I seem to have lost my appetite for now. If it wouldn't be too much trouble, could you have someone bring up a tray to my room later? I need to lie down."

Stephanie pushed her chair back and stood too. She looked incredibly regretful about her remark. "I apologize, Stella. Let me walk you up to your room."

THE TWO HAD BARELY EXITED the room when Trinity came through the side door from the kitchen, apron in hand, which she quickly donned and tied behind her back before hefting a dish-laden tray from the mahogany sideboard.

"Never again!" Trinity declared with a furious shake of her head, then, careful not to spill the contents, she carried a quintet of plates around the table, placing one on each carefully polished charger while the remaining family members still seated watched her in surprised silence.

"Have either of you ever heard the term *bridezilla*? I can well assure you my friend Vivianne—if she *is* still my friend after today—fits the stereotype to a T! There must surely be a picture of her to the side of any dictionary definition available to search."

Finished with her distribution of the afternoon meal, Trinity put down the tray and closed her eyes. Like Stella, she struggled for calm. "We weren't even in the bridal shop five minutes before she started *demanding* things. She wanted tea. Though the shop doesn't offer it, one of the custodians ordered from a local shop. Just for her. It was cold. She wanted hors d'oeuvres. She wanted champagne. She wanted blue undergarments to try beneath one of the gowns. She was brought blue and argued that they were aqua."

Reggie's brow rose, and a low whistle slipped from between his lips. "Sounds like you had a rough morning, Trin."

"Honestly, there was not one single thing with which she did not find fault—and she never hesitated to make her displeasure known. Loudly. I was so embarrassed to be there with her. One of the ladies in charge of bringing the wedding gowns asked my name, and I—I pretended not to hear her."

"Are you speaking of the same Vivianne we rescued a couple of months ago?" Araminta asked. "She didn't seem the type to be so demanding."

"The same, yes. If you had witnessed her behavior this morning, you would never believe it," Trinity told her. "I certainly had a hard time doing so."

"I'm afraid I don't understand—" Araminta started, but Trinity cut her off before she could finish.

"She says it's a matter of respect. As Mr. Roy's

bride-to-be, she believes she deserves the respect due one in her position, and she obviously did not think she was being shown the amount of respect she somehow deserves—due to her new position as Stephen Roy's fiancée—at the bridal shop today."

"Wait a minute, Trinity. Was she wearing an engagement ring?" Daisy asked.

Trinity's eyes widened. "Engagement ring? Ohhhh, yes. A big, gaudy, flashy marquis-cut diamond surrounded by sapphires on either side. Six, to be precise. She barely stopped looking at it the entire time I was there."

"Did she mention where it was purchased?"

"Belamie's, of course," Trinity said. "She was rather uppity about it too. That was right after she practically floored one of the sales assistants with a karate move for bringing the wrong shoes!"

Araminta made a mental note to call Ivan after lunch to see if he could verify a purchase from Belamie's. She waved Trinity over. "Why don't you join us, dear? Stella has decided she would prefer to have a tray in her room. You can sit in her place."

"I'm so sorry to have upset you, Stella," Stephanie apologized as soon as she and Stella were out of earshot of the dining room. "I know how hard losing Bart must be for you. Ivan told me what he did for you—I hope you don't mind."

Stella shook her head no. "Of course I don't mind. Bartholomew was a lovely man and his benevolence should be recognized. I will be forever grateful for his generosity, but I am not the only one he has helped, you know."

"If you mean the charities, I do know. He donated quite a substantial amount to the local shelter alongside what was raised by the cat show this week."

"And the homeless shelters. Soup kitchens. Bart was a caring, generous soul. Always giving things to people. I cannot understand why anyone would wish him harm."

Stephanie put her arm around Stella's shoulders and gave her a pat. "There, there. It is difficult, I know, but I think Bart would rather us do what we can to figure out who is responsible than to lock ourselves into mourning."

"He did love hardworking folks, didn't he?" Stella sniffed. "I am going to miss him so."

A flash and blur caught Stephanie's eye, but it was too late. Arun dashed between her and Stella, making both ladies stumble backward in surprise. Stephanie had barely balanced from the first whirlwind when Sasha, too, streaked behind Stella, sending her wobbling back toward Stephanie, who caught her arm, steadying her.

"What in the world?" She stared in wonder at the two cats racing for the stairs, then she glanced at the door to Stella's room. It was slightly ajar, just enough for a cat—or two cats, as the case seemed to be—to slip through.

"We'd best go inside and make sure they haven't shredded anything important," she told Stella.

Nothing seemed out of place at first glance, but when Stephanie stepped farther into the room, she saw Codger sitting on the antique cherry writing desk near the window, quietly licking his paw.

Hurrying to retrieve him in case he was sitting on something he shouldn't, she bent then carefully scooped him into her arms. "Oh, Codger, what are you doing in here?"

"He's fine," Stella insisted. She reached over and chucked Codger under his chin and crooned to him. "I don't mind their company. In fact, I find myself talking to them as I would speak with Bartholomew."

Stephanie laughed. "So does Aunt Minta, but don't tell her I said so. She doesn't seem to realize she's doing it sometimes, and we often catch her—Reggie and I—discussing everything from the weather to her wardrobe with Sasha and Arun."

To Codger, she said, "I'll take you to Minta. I'm sure she won't want you up here in the guest rooms, roaming at will."

Codger gave her a bored, disinterested look and stretched out, getting comfortable in her arms, and Stella laughed. "Looks like he's looking forward to the trip."

By the time Stephanie reached the main hallway, she was practically shaking with excitement. She had

55

managed to keep her composure in Stella's room, but now…

Bending, she let Codger down onto the floor then turned in a slow, happy circle, a huge smile wreathing her lips. "It's official! I am going to be engaged soon!"

After a few moments wherein one thought rapidly followed another—bridesmaids, flowers from the gardens, a white trellis of roses, a fountain, and Ivan looking at her with love in his eyes—Stephanie stopped spinning and started toward the dining room. She needed to tell Araminta she knew who Bertie's secret client was: Ivan!

When she'd scooped Codger off the desk, her gaze had caught a jeweler's receipt with the name Hershey scribbled on it in handwriting she recognized. She was so excited, she didn't know how she was going to keep what she'd learned to herself, but she must. Ivan hadn't even proposed yet!

Ivan hasn't even proposed yet.

She stopped, considering. Maybe she shouldn't mention it to Araminta yet. Keeping what she had learned to herself until Ivan let the cat out of the bag would be difficult enough. If her aunt knew the secret as well…

The thought had barely completed when her mind wandered onto another… and another. When *would* he propose? Had he planned to do it after the cat show? He was coming to the manor tomorrow. Maybe he would ask her then? No, he would probably wait until after Bart's murder was solved and his grandfather's name was cleared—wouldn't he? *Oh, dear, what should I wear?*

"I GUESS that didn't go exactly as planned," Arun said as they watched Stephanie stare off into space with a dreamy look in her eyes.

Sasha sighed. "She fixated on that one receipt, but what we really wanted to show was the lack of receipts."

"And our attempts to lead her to the room with the camera were thwarted with all her spinning and twirling about." Codger flicked his tail. "I'm glad she put me down. I was getting quite dizzy."

"At least we know one thing now," Sasha said. "Our little Stephanie has the same snooping gene as Araminta."

"Except in her case, she isn't finding any of the relevant clues." Arun preened his long whiskers.

"I suppose one should hardly blame her. It is quite exciting to know you will be proposed to. Apparently, all that hand holding under the table has paid off," Sasha said.

"There is one curious thing, though. How could young Ivan afford such a ring?" Arun asked,

Sasha thought for a bit. "Bertie was friends with Jacob. Perhaps he offered a special price or maybe a payment plan. I do hope it's not some sort of fake receipt. It seems young Stephanie has her heart set on a proposal."

"Okay, well, what's plan B?" Codger asked. "We need to get someone to find that camera. What do we do now?"

Arun trotted over to the top of the stairs and peered down through the banister. "Now, we wait for Araminta to come up, and we do whatever it takes to lead her to the camera."

CHAPTER SEVEN

*A*raminta slipped into Daisy's office with all three cats at her heels. They had been following her closely for the past half hour, since she'd gone to her room to grab a sweater. She was happy to see Codger in relatively good spirits as the cats tumbled down the hallway, playing with this and that and scratching at various doors, trying to get into the rooms. They certainly were being quite acrobatic, but Araminta thought their playful mood might be a bit tone-deaf. She didn't have time to indulge them, especially not when they seemed to have a particular obsession with one of the rooms. Jacob was still in jail, after all, and she was solely focused on finding the clues that would get him out.

In the office, she went around the desk to make her call. She asked for Ivan. While she waited to be connected, Codger jumped up on the desk and stared at her with his golden eyes. She sensed sadness in them

59

and maybe even a bit of gratitude to her for caring for him. She reached out and petted him. "Don't worry. Jacob will be home soon."

Once upon a time, she had thought Codger might be a permanent part of her life, just as Sasha and Arun had become. They would be a family. With Jacob. Once upon a time, she had dreamed of having a family of her own, but life had become complicated, and time had continued to pass. Now…

"Ivan Hershey. How may I help you?"

Ivan's voice snapped Araminta out of her thoughts. "I need you to check on something for me regarding Stephen Roy. I have it on good authority that his fiancée is wearing a Belamie ring, yet Jacob told me Bertie had refused to sell to the man. If you could possibly verify his purchase, I can clear him from my list of question-able interests."

"And if I cannot verify it?" Ivan asked. "I'm going to need a warrant, and since I'm not on the case offi-cially, that might be difficult." He sounded distracted and sad.

"True. Well, maybe I will have to visit Stephen Roy and ask for the receipt…"

"I don't think that's a good idea. You could get hurt, Araminta. Do you think my grandfather would ever forgive me if I allowed something to happen to you?" There was a strain in his voice. Araminta knew he was imagining just such a scenario, and he did not like what he had conjured in his thoughts.

"Precisely, dear boy, and that is why you should do

everything you can to aid me in figuring out who is truly responsible for Bertie's death. We need Jacob home again, safe and sound, and since you can't be in the forefront of this investigation, perhaps it would put you in good stead with your grandfather if you quietly stepped up and led from the background."

Araminta ended the call with those words and leaned back in the chair. She understood Ivan's predicament with being recused from the case and not being able to follow up on things. Jacob would never let something like that stop him. Ivan was no Jacob, though, but maybe this case and her strong words would help him find the courage to be more like his grandfather.

Before she could dwell on it further, Daisy came inside. "Oh! I didn't know you were in here. If you're busy with something, I can wait."

Araminta rose and waved her words away. "Just a phone call, and I've finished it."

Daisy walked to the desk while Araminta headed for the door. She caught the scent of flowers and freshly mown grass, and she remembered something Reggie had told her. "Daisy, the night Bertie was murdered, did you let Codger out on the side lawn?"

"Hm?" Daisy asked, busy with a sheaf of papers she'd brought with her to her desk. "Oh, no. I wouldn't do that. I thought he was in the dining room with the rest of us."

"He was at first, but…"

"You've thought of something?" Daisy asked, the papers forgotten for now.

"Possibly." Araminta nodded. "Reggie said Codger was on the side lawn when he came home that night. Someone must have let him out."

"You're right!" Daisy said. "But who would have done that?"

"I'm not sure," Araminta told her. "But I think we need to find out."

A QUARTER OF AN HOUR LATER, the entire staff of Moorecliff Manor and the Moorecliff family were assembled in the front parlor. The only person in the manor not in attendance for the meeting was Stella, who was resting in her room.

"Reggie saw Codger outside the night of the murder, and I was wondering if one of you let him out and, if so, perhaps saw something that could be of use in the investigation," Araminta said gently. She didn't want it to appear as if she were accusing any of the staff; she knew none of them were murderers. "It would've been somewhere between seven twenty and seven thirty."

Everyone shrugged and looked at each other.

"I was in the dining room with the rest of you," Trinity said.

"I was in the mudroom with…" Harold let his voice trail off.

"I was taking a tray up to Mr. Roy in his room." Mary, the cook, scrunched her face up as if trying to remember. "I came through the foyer to the stairs. Miss Vivianne and Miss Stella were at the front door, but I didn't see Codger."

"They were?" Araminta remembered Stella saying she had wanted to see Daryl Sendquist out, but did Vivianne know him too? "Was the reporter there too?"

"No. Just the two of them, but I suppose he could have just left. I do believe Stella was shutting the door."

"Codger might've slipped out," Trinity said. "Vivianne is a little disorganized and not very observant. You should've seen her throwing her things into her suitcase as she was leaving. Stuff was flying everywhere. And at the bridal shop, she just tossed dresses about and then demanded someone find them again. She probably wouldn't notice the cat slipping out." Trinity rolled her eyes, still thinking about the bridezilla incident.

Harold cleared his throat. "The front door isn't the only way Codger could get out. There are many doors in this mansion."

"And the mudroom is one of them. Perhaps Codger had been in there when the murder happened," Daisy said.

Trinity gasped. "That would mean that the murderer let him out!"

"Yes, but let's not get ahead of ourselves. First, we should talk to Vivianne and Stella. But Stella doesn't seem keen to open up to any of us. Perhaps we could get Ivan to get something out of her," Araminta suggested, and Stephanie's eyes went wide.

"Why do you think Ivan could get her to talk?" Stephanie asked. Araminta thought her tone was a bit defensive. "Just because he was one of Bart's customers doesn't mean Stella will be willing to open up to Ivan about his murder."

Araminta pinned her with a narrowed gaze. "Ivan was a customer?"

Stephanie bit at her lip. Too late, she realized she had revealed too much. She nodded. "He was."

"How do you know, dear?" Daisy asked her. "He hasn't said one word about it to either of us, and given the nature of this case, it seems he would have."

Stephanie shrugged. "I suppose so… unless he was trying to keep a secret, right?"

Araminta was confused. "What kind of secret would he keep during a murder investigation, Steph?"

"Oh, I don't know," she said and shrugged again. Her cheeks were suddenly flushed, and she seemed hesitant to meet her aunt's or her stepmother's gaze. "Perhaps the purchase of an engagement ring?"

CHAPTER EIGHT

*A*n engagement ring! Araminta hadn't thought of that. In fact, such an idea had been farthest from her mind. If Ivan had proposed, Jacob would know. Wouldn't he? Surely, Ivan would have mentioned it. "Stephanie, are you telling us Ivan has proposed marriage?"

Stephanie quickly shook her head. "Oh, no. Not yet. I mean—"

Daisy was frowning, motioning with her hand for the staff to give them privacy. She waited until the door closed behind Harold then said, "I don't understand, Stephanie, dear. If Ivan hasn't broached the matter of a proposal to you, how would you know anything about his purchase of an engagement ring from Mr. Belamie?"

A miserable groan escaped Stephanie just before she sat down in a chair near her stepmother. "I've made an utter hash of this, haven't I?"

"Out with it, Steph," Reggie insisted, though he rested a comforting hand on her shoulder. "Unless you want us to start thinking you're covering up something for your precious police investigator."

"I'd never do that!" Stephanie blurted, aghast.

"Then you should tell us what you know and how you came by the information. Quickly, if you please," Reggie told her.

Araminta nodded in agreement.

"I-I saw his name on a jeweler's receipt in Stella's room," she said, her expression one of shamed misery. "Yesterday, when I walked up with Stella, Codger dashed in there. Sasha and Arun, too, of course. But Codger, he was sitting on a desk on top of what I thought could be important papers, and when I lifted him up to bring him out, I saw it."

Araminta struggle to fit Stephanie's revelation with everything else. How could Ivan's purchase of a ring have anything to do with Bertie?

"But when did he buy this ring? Did he meet with Bertie yesterday?" Araminta asked. If he had, then why had he not said anything?

Stephanie thought for a minute then shook her head. "He must have bought it before then. I met him at the door, Aunt Minta. We came straight to the dining room, where we joined the rest of you. There was no time for him to have met Bertie in the mudroom. I should have checked the date on the receipt."

"Shouldn't he be asking me for your hand? I mean

with Dad gone, I guess I am the man of the family," Reggie teased.

Something in his tone seemed to make Stephanie bristle. "Well, how could he when you're traveling about the world all the time?"

Reggie laughed. "Don't go getting your dander up, sis. I'm not about to start playing overprotective brother at this late date. Your Ivan is safe from me."

"But not from me," Daisy said, an edge of seriousness gilding her usually soothing tone. "If that boy has intentions, Stephanie, I'd like to think he would come to me—out of respect for Archie, of course."

Stephanie's brow wrinkled. "I don't know what to say, Daisy. I'm almost sorry I saw the receipt now. Please... don't mention any of this to Ivan. I don't want him to think I go around snooping..."

Reggie's laughter spilled into the room. "Stephanie, darling, in case you've forgotten—Ivan has met all of us, Aunt Minta included. Don't you think he would be well aware that you have snooping in your blood?"

"Still, I really would hate to out this secret before he is ready, Reginald." Stephanie emphasized her brother's full name and shot him a warning glance.

Reggie sat back in his chair, his usual impish grin on his face. "Don't worry, sis. He won't hear it from me."

Stephanie raised her brows at Araminta and Daisy.

"Us either," they both said.

Araminta smiled, partly to reassure her grandniece that her secret was safe and partly because Stephanie had just possibly given her another clue. If Stella kept receipts in her room, then she might have the one that would clear Stephen Roy. If she didn't have one from him, well… maybe then Mr. Roy would stay pegged at the top of Araminta's suspect list.

"I'M SORRY, Araminta, but Bixcombe is keeping everything close to the vest," Ivan told Araminta later over her phone. It was one of those face chat things Reggie had shown her. Poor Ivan looked pretty down in the dumps and not at all like a man who was about to pop the question. Nor had he mentioned anything about buying a ring himself, even though Araminta had dropped a few hints. He'd had plenty of opportunity while telling her he had had no luck getting a peek at the receipts to verify Stephen Roy had purchased one. Maybe Steph had been mistaken about the receipt. Or perhaps he had bought jewelry from Bertie, but just not an engagement ring… Or if he did, maybe it wasn't for Steph.

"I haven't made much progress either." Araminta told him about Codger being outside and her suspicions about Vivianne and, now, Stella. "I still need to talk to this Daryl Sendquist." She refrained from mentioning that she also intended to snoop in Stella's room for the receipts. Saying it out loud made it seem that much worse.

"Grandfather has the utmost confidence in you in such matters," Ivan told her.

No pressure there. Araminta knew he meant the words to be a comfort, but they only made her feel more incompetent than she already did. Why was this particular case so confusing?

"We mustn't allow our emotions to get involved," Ivan reminded her. "Follow the clues and only the clues."

Tears burned because he'd sounded so much like Jacob, but she forced them away. "The clues, yes. But we have so few, and we've looked into them all. If only we could find out more about Vivianne's ring."

"We need a socialite, someone with connections. There's a big party coming up at the Ruemont Estate, and I'm sure Stephen and Vivianne will be there," Ivan said. "We could wire them up and send them in undercover. See if we can find out about the ring."

Araminta's eyes narrowed. "Would Bixcombe agree to that, or does he think he already has the killer in custody?"

Ivan lowered his voice and leaned toward his computer. "He might not agree, but some of the other detectives would be willing to do it behind his back. None of them believe that Grandfather could have done this. But we don't have anyone to send in."

Araminta's eyes widened. "Oh but, I think I do! Oh, Ivan, bless you, we do have just such a person. In fact, we have a couple who will do nicely. I'll need an engagement ring, though, preferably one from Belamie's."

69

"I could probably get one, but who are you thinking you'd send in?"

Araminta grinned. "Why, Reginald Moorecliff, of course. Vivianne won't recognize him; they've never met. He is perfect and would be especially delighted to do the deed."

"But… you said a couple."

Araminta nodded. "I'll send Stephanie in with him. In disguise, of course. She will play his newly affianced girlfriend."

Ivan was shaking his head side to side. "No. I will not allow it. I won't have Stephanie put herself in danger…"

"You'd not deny her this chance to prove she is as capable of taking care of herself as you, now would you, Ivan? Besides, Reggie would never allow his sister to be harmed. She will be in the best of hands. Plus your department will have them wired, and I'm sure you'll be standing by," she reminded him.

Excitement stirred in her breast, and she could almost feel her eyes sparkling with anticipation of the coming event as well as pride for Ivan's courage to go behind Bixcombe's back and consider an undercover operation. Now that she had something to do to help further her investigation, she would not allow Ivan to talk her out of going through with it. "I think it is the perfect plan!"

CHAPTER NINE

"She's coming out of her room!" Sasha meowed as Araminta stepped into the hallway.

"Now is our chance!" Arun rushed over to Araminta and weaved around her ankles.

"Well, hello, dear. Yes, I have been a bit busy. Are you in need of petting?" Araminta tried to pick him up, but Arun dashed away toward Codger, who was lying listlessly in the hallway.

Codger let out a pitiful meow, swished his tail, and rolled onto his side. Araminta rushed over to tend to him, just as they'd figured she would. Codger let her pet him once but then leaped up and trotted down the hallway toward the wing that housed the guest rooms.

"Oh dear... he looks out of sorts." Araminta followed, and Arun and Sasha would have high-fived each other if they'd had hands instead of paws.

71

Codger trotted past the grand stairway and into the guest wing.

"Where are you going?" Araminta asked. "Here, kitty, do you want some tuna?"

Codger didn't stop as he headed toward the room where they'd found the camera.

"What is he up to?" Araminta eyed Arun and Sasha.

"I think she might be on to us," Sasha said.

"About time." Arun's eyes slitted as Araminta stopped in front of Stella's room. The door was cracked open, and Araminta peered in through the crack before looking back behind her and quietly pushing the door wider.

"Hey, over here!" Codger meowed from the doorway to the room with the camera, which was next to Stella's room. "Why is she going in there?"

Arun sighed. "Who knows? One can never be sure what our Araminta is up to."

Arun and Sasha trotted over to join Codger in the doorway.

"Should we go in and get her?" Sasha asked.

Arun shook his head. "I say we wait and try to grab her when she comes out."

"THOSE CLEVER CATS!" Araminta thought as she tiptoed into Stella's room. They must have known that Stella was out and that she wanted to look at the receipts and led her straight to the room. She made a mental note to have Mary provide a special treat for them later.

The room was neat as a pin. Stella must be very organized, which made sense. She would have to be to assist Bertie. The bed was neatly made, and no clothing was flung about. A quick peek into the bathroom showed all her toiletries lined up neatly on the vanity.

Now where should I look for the receipts? Araminta turned and spied the antique cherry writing desk. *Yes!* Stephanie had said Codger was atop the desk, lying on the receipts. Hopefully they were still there.

Keeping one ear cocked toward the hallway lest Stella return, she hurried over to the desk.

She was in luck. The receipts were still there, stacked in a tidy pile. Araminta shuffled through them. Broadcliff, Smith, Cantorelli... Nothing from Stephen Roy. She did, however, see the Hershey receipt. So Stephanie wasn't mistaken. But why hadn't Ivan mentioned anything? She dearly hoped the ring really was for Steph. The poor girl would be heartbroken, and with the way the two carried on, her opinion of Ivan would be greatly lowered if he had another girl on the side.

A cat scratched at the door, and Araminta heard someone coming up the stairs. *Oh no!* It was Stella talking on her phone.

Araminta slipped into the hallway, but it sounded like Stella was just about to turn the corner. She could pretend she was down there tending to another room, but what if Stella was the killer? She might suspect

Araminta was nosing around in her room and flee, or worse, make Araminta her next victim.

A hiss caught her attention, and she turned to see the three cats standing in the door of the room next to Stella's. The door was ajar, and Codger ran in. Arun twitched his tail, and Sasha meowed, except it sounded like she'd said, "In here!"

Good idea! Araminta ran into the room.

The three cats were sitting next to the bed, staring at her expectantly.

"Shhh…" Araminta put her finger to her lips as she quietly closed the door. "What are you three up to?"

"Meow!" Sasha rubbed her face on Araminta's calf.

"Meroop." Codger swished his bushy tail. He looked like he was doing much better.

"Good to see you feel better, Codger," Araminta whispered. "Not to worry, Jacob will be home soon."

But as Araminta said the words, she wondered, *Will he be home soon?* She'd done a fair amount of detecting, but the identity of the killer still eluded her. Except it was very telling that Stella did not have a receipt from Stephen Roy. Perhaps this little undercover operation tonight would be the thing that finally pulled the case together.

"Mewoop!" Arun disappeared under the bed.

"What in the world are you doing?" Araminta asked.

Sasha and Codger follow Arun.

"I guess I'd better look under the bed." Araminta got to her knees and peered under. Three sets of luminescent cat's eyes blinked back at her. They were sitting in a row, and in front of them was a small digital camera.

"Will you look at that!" Araminta reached under and pulled it out. "Where did this come from?"

The cats didn't answer, but Araminta wasn't expecting one. Her mind was already racing ahead. Vivianne and Stephen had stayed in this room. Did the camera belong to them? Trinity had said Vivianne wasn't very neat. Had she dropped it and not realized? Araminta would have to return it, of course. Maybe she could use that as an excuse to glean more information about the ring.

Ping!

Araminta looked at her phone. A message from Stephanie told her that she was dressed and ready for the undercover operation.

Araminta turned to the cats. "I better put this in my room and dash out—no time to look at it now, but thank you!"

She opened the door slowly and, upon seeing that the coast was clear, rushed down the hall to her room.

CHAPTER TEN

Stephanie picked at the dark wig her aunt had provided. Araminta could see the uncertainty in her eyes before she asked, "Are you sure this will work, Aunt Minta?"

"Of course it will work, darling," she assured her. "Just flash that ring around and croon to Reggie about how you never expected to receive such a prize. Vivianne will hear you, and she will no doubt want to prove her own ring to be superior, then you can get more details about when and where it was purchased."

"Your disguise will ensure that Mr. Roy and Vivianne do not recognize you," Daisy told her. "Neither of them were in your immediate presence for very long."

"But what if I say the wrong thing? What if I'm not convincing enough? What if no one believes that anyone would give me an engagement ring?"

77

"But you were just bragging how Ivan had bought you a ring at Belamie's." Reggie made a face.

"I wasn't bragging," Stephanie shot back, then her face fell. "But he hasn't proposed yet, even though I've hinted around."

"Maybe it's just taking him some time, dear," Daisy soothed.

"Or maybe he changed his mind." Stephanie sounded so dejected that Araminta wanted to do something. Usually, the girl oozed confidence. She must really be in love with Ivan. But Araminta had seen the receipt, and the amount was in keeping with a very expensive engagement ring. Why hadn't he said anything to Stephanie? *It couldn't possibly be for someone else…*

Araminta didn't want to think about that. She couldn't bear to see her grandniece's heart broken. She decided to turn the conversation to the undercover matter at hand. Pulling that off would bring back Stephanie's confidence and cheerful demeanor.

"All in due time, dear. Besides, remember you don't need any man to make you happy," Araminta said to Stephanie.

Stephanie smiled. "True. You're always so wise."

Araminta beamed at the compliment. "Now we have business to attend to. Remember that while you two are mingling with the elite criminal crowd who are sure to be in attendance tonight, along with the others."

Araminta pinned a white microphone disguised beneath a flower onto Stephanie's purse. "Now go

78

downstairs and find out if Ivan and the detectives have arrived with your new temporary ring."

IVAN GLANCED at his watch and then at the stairwell. Harold had escorted him to the front parlor to wait for Stephanie, Reggie, and Araminta, but he'd been far too agitated to sit and wait patiently for the trio to put in an appearance. Instead, he'd moved to the foyer to pace until they came down.

He was worried about Stephanie. Worried Stephen Roy would realize who Reginald was, though he had not met him. Surely someone from Tony Romano's gang would know him?

The very real possibility of either Moorecliff sibling being outed weighed on his conscience. How could he allow them to put themselves in such a dangerous scenario?

His desire to clear his grandfather had overtaken his normally sensible thinking. Even agreeing to this unsanctioned surveillance was so unlike him. But detectives Rutherford and Crosby had insisted they knew Jacob was innocent, too, and this might be the only way to get evidence to convince Bixcombe. According to Rutherford, Bixcombe had run into a few snags building his case against Jacob, and new information about Bertie's assistant, Stella, had come to light.

"Hello, Ivan," Stephanie said, her smile beaming. He would know her anywhere, of course, but he had to admit the stylish gown, heels, and dark-red wig in an upswept do definitely gave her an air of mystery and intrigue.

He swallowed hard and nodded. "Miss Moorecliff. Stephanie. You look very beautiful in your disguise."

If it were possible, her smile became more radiant. She twirled in front of him. "Isn't it gorgeous? Daisy lent me a few things."

Ivan refrained from commenting on the clothing. Instead, he asked, "And the wig?"

Reginald, who had come downstairs behind his sister in elegant evening attire, pulled at his cuffs and smiled. "Aunt Minta, of course. She does seem to be prepared for any occasion."

"Of course," Ivan agreed, nodding. He turned to Stephanie and held out his hand for hers. "May I?"

She placed her hand in his palm, and he took something from his pocket. The ring. His eyes met hers as he slid it onto her finger. She did not look away until Reggie cleared his throat.

"Shouldn't we get a move on? This gala thing starts in twenty minutes," he reminded them before the whole ring thing could evolve into a mushy moment he didn't care to witness.

"Good thinking, Reggie," Araminta said, finally making her own appearance at the top of the stairs. "We don't want to be late."

Stephanie scoffed. "Have you forgotten, Auntie? Being late is a mark of utmost fashionability. Whenever we arrive, we shall be right on time."

CHAPTER ELEVEN

The inside of the surveillance van parked discreetly outside the Ruemont estate, where the fundraiser gala Stephanie and Reginald were attending was being held, was cramped and noisy. Araminta harrumphed as she wiggled herself into the only seat available for her, but she took it and kept her complaints quiet.

Detectives Rutherford and Crosby were renegades at the police department. They never played by the rules, so when they'd commandeered the older surveillance van for a covert operation, no one downtown had batted an eye. Luckily, the two detectives had worked with Jacob when they were new on the force and had the utmost respect for him.

"I hope we get something good on here to prove Roy is the culprit. It would be a coup to put him behind bars and prove Mr. Hershey's innocence at the same time," Rutherford said as he put the headphones on.

81

"True. And taking Bixcombe down a notch would be the icing on the cake." Crosby's reply earned him a high-five from the other detective.

The detectives spent a few minutes tuning the equipment. Unfortunately, there wasn't enough equipment in the old van for everyone, so Ivan and Araminta couldn't listen in.

While Araminta was not happy with his directive, she agreed with the terms, but only because she knew she would be privy to everything later since she had slipped the tiny recorder into the flower she'd attached to Steph's purse.

Ivan sidled into the seat beside her. "Well, Araminta, is this little stakeout of ours everything you thought it would be?"

"This isn't my first stakeout, you know. I just hope Stephanie takes to playing the role of an engaged person," Araminta hinted, curious to see Ivan's reaction.

"What do you mean?"

Araminta picked at a piece of lint on her black polyester trousers. Instead of her usual colorful ensemble, she'd opted for an entirely black outfit, which seemed more fitting for surveillance. "Well, she mentioned some nerves at playing the role. Thinking people might not believe anyone would ask her to marry them."

Leaning back in his seat, Ivan crossed his arms over his chest and studied Araminta as if trying to read between the lines of what she was saying. She raised a brow, hoping that would move him along. The boy certainly wasn't as sharp as his grandfather when it came to subtext.

Then, as if lightning had struck some hazy portion of his brain, he sat forward, got up, and went to Crosby in the front of the van. "Is this Miss Stephanie's feed?"

Crosby nodded.

Ivan held out his hand for his headset. "May I? This will only take a moment."

Crosby gave him a doubtful look, but then he shrugged and handed the gear over to Ivan.

Without looking at Araminta, Ivan settled the thing on his head. "Stephanie? Can you hear me?"

No one other than Ivan could hear her reply, but she must have given one, because he continued to speak. "Look, I know this is neither the time nor the place, and is likely highly inappropriate, given the circumstances, but... Stephanie Moorecliff, will you marry me?"

INSIDE RUEMONT HOUSE, Stephanie went still. To her credit, she never touched her earpiece. "Excuse me? Wait. Say that again?"

Reggie gave her a curious look, then he was even more befuddled when she suddenly grinned.

"He wants to marry me!" she whispered.

Unfortunately, her excited explanation came at an inopportune moment of silence from the surrounding crowd. To make matters worse, she stood up and reached for Reggie's hands. Then, practically bouncing in place, she repeated the phrase once again, only louder. "He wants to marry me!"

A voice spoke up in Reggie's ear. "Stay calm. It seems our boy decided now was the perfect moment to propose. I'm seeing a bit of confusion, but…"

The crowd started to clap and cheer. Reggie took his cue from the moment and stood with a grin on his lips. "Of course I do, darling. Why else would I have given you such an exquisite engagement ring?"

Stephanie wrapped her arms around his neck and hugged him, then she stepped back. Holding one hand up, she stared at the ring then up at Reggie. "It is exquisite, darling. In fact, it is perfect! I never imagined owning something so beautiful," she said, her words easily heard over the low murmur of the now-settled crowd. "But then, when you purchase a Belamie jewel, it could be nothing less."

From the corner of his eye, Reggie saw a woman stand and motion to her companion, who also stood. Quietly, he said, "They are moving."

Seconds later, Vivianne stood beside their table, her arm possessively looped through Stephen Roy's. "Pardon me, did you say you're also wearing a Belamie ring?" Vivianne asked. She extended her left hand to show off a large diamond-and-sapphire ring.

Stephanie nodded and held up her own. The motion seemed all the encouragement Vivianne needed to invite herself and her companion to be seated at their table. "If you don't mind the intrusion, I would love to hear your story."

"Story?" Stephanie asked, momentarily confused.

It was Reggie who saved the day. Leaning toward Stephanie, he took her hand in his, patted it, then explained what Vivianne meant. "Your *ring* story, darling," he prompted.

Reggie grinned at Stephen Roy, and said, "With the ladies, there is *always* a story about the ring."

CHAPTER TWELVE

On the ride back to the manor, Araminta was practically beside herself with anticipation. Vivianne had spent the better part of an hour with her niece and nephew. Unfortunately, only the detectives had been privy to the conversation. They'd been disappointed with what they'd heard and claimed that neither Stephen nor Viv had given up any good information, but Araminta wasn't about to lose hope. She could hardly wait to retrieve the recorder from Stephanie's purse and hear every juicy detail of what had been said for herself.

"The Ruemont place is lovely, Aunt Minta," Stephanie said, attempting a bit of small talk for the ride back to the manor. "Have you visited?"

"Of course. Years ago, Talila Ruemont and I spent an entire summer down at the lake house."

Jacob had been there, as well, Araminta recalled, though she did not share that memory with her niece and nephew. She hadn't known he would be present at the time, but when Talila's brother, Fredrick, showed up at the lake with his rowing partner, it had been all Araminta could do to keep her heels on the ground. As a young man, Jacob had caused quite a stir with the ladies, and Araminta had been one of them.

"I never knew you and 'Lila were friends," Reggie said. "It must have been difficult for you when she passed away."

Araminta nodded. That was the year she had moved into Moorecliff Manor with Archibald, and Reggie was right, of course. Losing one of her dear friends had been especially trying. "It was a long time ago, my dears, and we shouldn't be dragging our feet by reminiscing on old times while another of our close friends is being forced to cool his heels in a cell downtown."

Though Araminta would not admit it if asked, memories of her summer at Ruemont struck a special nerve just now because that was the summer before she'd gone off to explore the world, the summer before Jacob had joined the police academy. It was also the summer Jacob Hershey had asked her to marry him... and she had turned him down.

"Stephen Roy is not at all what I expected to find as the new crime boss. Are you sure your information is correct, Aunt Minta?" Reggie asked.

"As it came direct from the horse's mouth, I believe I shall say yes, Reginald. But you've made me curious now. Just what kind of man did you expect him to be?"

Reggie shrugged. "I figured he would likely be a younger, tougher copy of Tony Romano."

"He seems sweet," Stephanie said, then she shrugged in apology when three pairs of eyes turned on her in surprise. "Well, he does. Even at the manor, he seemed genuinely interested in Vivianne's happiness. And, Aunt Araminta, you have to admit he took great care of his cat."

"You will stay away from him, Stephanie," Ivan told her. "Crime bosses do not become such by being sweet. You've no idea what the man is likely capable of."

"Hmph," Araminta grumbled. "Barely engaged, and already, the boy is trying to tell you what to do, Steph."

Stephanie looked at Ivan and grinned. "Isn't it wonderful? And the way he proposed... I don't think I shall ever forget it."

Reggie snorted. "The *proposal* story. Right. Your guy asked you to marry him in the middle of a tension-fraught stakeout with a crime boss and his girlfriend and two amateurs at the helm. If I did not know how serious all this is, I would deem our lives perfect for a reality TV show. What about you, Aunt Minta? Do you think you could still solve murders if you had to do it with cameras in your face and people following you around everywhere?"

The horror his idea invoked must have been evident on her face, because he laughed again, and this time, Stephanie and Ivan joined in.

"I wouldn't dream of doing any such thing," she

told them. But after a moment's quiet reflection on the matter, she lifted her gaze once more. "You know…"

"No!"

A trio of negativity shot down the thought before it had fully formed in her thoughts. Not that she had been serious. It was Araminta's time to laugh—a real, genuine laugh. And she enjoyed it.

The car slowed to a stop as they pulled up in front of the manor. Ivan got out and assisted Stephanie while Reggie did the same from the other side of the vehicle for Araminta. To his aunt, he said, "We should go on inside. I think those two have some things to talk about that neither of us probably care to hear."

"Just one second." Araminta walked around the car to Stephanie and Ivan. "I know you two have things to discuss. If you want, I can carry your things inside. I'll leave them with Harold so you can collect them when you come inside."

Stephanie, distracted no doubt by her anticipation of her time alone with Ivan, handed over her purse and wrap.

Araminta took the items and turned to Ivan. "Now I suppose you can present her with that ring."

"Ring? I don't actually have a ring." Ivan turned to Stephanie. "But don't worry. We'll get you one right away."

CHAPTER THIRTEEN

*A*raminta's mind raced as she hurried inside. If Ivan didn't have a ring, then why was there a receipt in Stella's room? Was Ivan just saying that so he could surprise Stephanie? Steph hadn't been fazed by his admission, even though she'd seen the receipt too. Maybe it had been for something else and he'd already told her when Araminta wasn't paying attention.

Or was something more nefarious going on? Bertie wouldn't want it known that he'd sold a ring to Stephen Roy, but what if Stephen had bought a ring and Bertie simply put another name on it so no one would know? But why Hershey? Jacob would not be happy to learn that Bertie had used his name as a fake receipt, but would he be mad enough to kill? And what good would a fake receipt be anyway? Perhaps Bertie needed something for his tax records.

As if sensing her thoughts, the three cats followed

91

along, each of them letting out a soft meow as they reached the room.

Araminta was so busy thinking that she hardly noticed Reggie also following her until she hooked the recorder from the flower to the computer in Daisy's office.

Arun jumped on the desk and batted at the small device she'd just inserted into the USB port.

"Meow!" Sasha hopped onto the bookcase.

Codger remained at her feet, but his eyes watched her intently.

"Okay, guys, let's see what Stephen Roy had to say for himself." Araminta picked Codger up and smiled at Reggie as she petted the cat.

"If you were fishing for evidence to clear Jacob at a public gala event, I can tell you, you are wasting your time. Stephanie and I heard nothing in our conversation with Mr. Roy and his fiancée that would lead us to believe he had anything to do with Bertie's murder."

"Meroo." Codger sounded disappointed.

Araminta gave Reggie a look. "Perhaps I will connect something in the conversation the two of you did not."

"Even if you do, won't the recording be inadmissible as evidence?"

"I don't intend it to be evidence. I just need to get an idea of where to dig for something that is."

A knock drew their attention. Harold opened the door. "Everyone is in the front parlor. Ms. Daisy has asked me to go to the cellar for a bottle of Moorecliff's best champagne. Will the two of you be joining them?"

Reggie looked to Araminta, one brow arched high. "Yes, shall we be joining the happy couple, Aunt?"

Araminta flashed a smile at Harold. Reggie, she ignored. "We will join everyone in the parlor directly, Harold. Thank you."

"You're not going to listen first?" Reggie asked his aunt.

Araminta looked at the device regretfully, as did Arun, Sasha, and Codger. "It will have to wait. This is Stephanie's grand moment, and I would never deny her the happiness of sharing with family."

Reggie walked beside her toward the parlor. Just before they reached the door, he leaned close and said, "You would never deny her the moment, but I'll wager you will be champing at the bit for whatever speech those two are about to give to be over!"

Before his aunt could reprimand him for his scampish behavior, Reggie hurried into the parlor with a big grin on his face. "Congratulations, sis! Ivan, welcome to the family."

"CHAMPAGNE?" Sasha turned up her delicate nose. "I will never understand why humans drink that vile stuff. Makes my whiskers tingle."

Codger shook his head as he glared in at the crowd in the parlor. They were all gathered around Stephanie and Ivan, who were beaming like someone had plugged them in.

"It's a celebration, and that's what humans like to drink," Arun said. "Personally, I prefer cream."

"How can they be celebrating when Jacob is still in jail?" Codger asked.

"I'm sure the celebration is dampened with that knowledge," Arun said. "See the tight lines around Ivan's eyes? He has not forgotten what is at stake."

"And Araminta seems anxious to get on with the investigation," Sasha said. "Still, I think it is nice they can have some joy during these trying times."

"Joy *schmoy*." Codger looked disgusted. "We need to get Araminta to look on that camera."

"And listen to the recording," Arun added.

"But Reggie said there was nothing on that recording. He was at the party and didn't hear anything of importance," Codger said.

"*He* didn't, but maybe our Araminta will notice something. She has skills for picking out clues that Reggie does not," Arun said.

"Perhaps," Codger said as Trinity came down the hall with a tray full of hors d'oeuvres.

Sasha's eyes brightened, and Arun thought he heard her stomach growl.

"I hope there is some cheese on that tray. We may need to mingle with the humans and see if we can grab some," Sasha said.

Arun glanced at Codger. Judging by Codger's raised brow, he'd also noticed that perhaps Sasha needed to lay off the cheese. Arun sent him a warning look before he could say anything to the finicky female feline. Poor Codger had no idea the damage Sasha could inflict with her claws when she was slighted.

Sasha was already on Trinity's heels, so Arun and Codger followed her into the room, hoping the human celebration would be a short one so they could get back to helping Araminta investigate without much delay.

IN THE END, it was Daisy who sat with Araminta to listen to the recording. When the conversation ended, Daisy made a sympathetic face. "I am sorry, Araminta. It doesn't sound like there was anything useful on there."

The cats seemed to disagree, judging by their loud meows, but Araminta hadn't picked up on anything either. Stephen had been skillfully evasive when Steph asked about when and where he'd bought the ring. He'd steered the conversation to other matters like their honeymoon plans, Viv's wheatgrass smoothie recipe, and her workout and self-defense training schedule.

When Reggie pressed him for details on the ring, he avoided giving specifics, which Araminta thought suspicious in itself. He'd vaguely said that he'd left it all up to Viv since she would be wearing it for the rest of her life.

"Stephen was very adept at avoiding the questions, wasn't he?" Araminta said.

"Probably learned that skill in his line of work,"

Daisy said. "All in all, the conversation was a bit boring."

At one point, the four had discussed Vivianne's love of photography. Since Tony's unfortunate removal and Viv's promotion, she'd apparently acquired a number of expensive cameras and pieces of photography equipment. Stephen, of course, had denied her nothing her heart might desire, including her fascination with historical houses like the Ruemont. She delighted in taking pictures of the various rooms and architectural elements in old houses.

"That does remind me, though. I found a camera under the bed in the room that Vivianne and Stephen occupied. We should probably contact her to return it," Araminta said.

Daisy frowned. "What were you doing under the bed in that room?"

"Oh, err... the cats." Araminta pointed toward Arun and Sasha, who sat proudly next to the door. "Whenever they indicate for me to look somewhere, I listen."

"Meow!" Arun said.

"Well, I guess we'd better turn in. It's late." Araminta rose and gave Daisy a hug. "Thanks for listening with me."

"You're welcome, and don't worry—you'll figure out who the killer is and free Jacob." Daisy started toward the doorway then stopped short. "Oh, and that reminds me. I got the number for Daryl Sendquist for you."

Araminta took the piece of paper. "Thanks. Maybe he'll provide us with the lead that we need."

Sasha and Arun followed Araminta to her room. Codger was waiting for them inside. He'd found a nice empty corner on a ledge on her dresser and was curled up around a figurine. He lifted his head in acknowledgment of her return then promptly laid his head back down to sleep. His fur was bedraggled, and his normally luminescent eyes lacked spark.

"I suppose you miss your master." Araminta petted Codger's fur.

She felt sure Codger understood because he lifted his head again to give her a look of withering disdain. "I see. I have it backward, do I? You are the master. Well, my apologies, good sir."

Apparently mollified, Codger settled once more, purring loudly enough now for the vibrations to be heard across the room. Araminta chuckled then reached down to scoop Sasha into her arms. She went to the bed and sat on the edge, and Arun jumped up beside her for a bit of cuddling, which she gave without hesitation.

After a moment, she sighed. "What are we to do, my pets?"

"Meow!" Arun jumped on the desk and batted at the camera.

"Do you want me to look on there?"

"Meroo!" Both Arun and Sasha answered. Codger slitted one eye open.

"Hmmm, that seems like an invasion of privacy." Araminta eyed the digital camera. It was a long shot, but there might be something useful on there, and it was no more an invasion than recording a conversation. She would only take a little peek…

She picked up the camera and looked through the small screen that showed the current photos. They must have been the ones Vivianne took at the cat show. She saw a closeup of some of the cats, then some pictures of guests, and one of Arun sitting pretty on the stone wall.

Wait a minute!

She stopped at a picture of Maisie Perkins. She looked smart in a tailored navy blue suit, smiling despite the walker in front of her. But Araminta wasn't looking at the walker. She was looking at the diamond-and-pearl clasp on her necklace. Araminta was sure it was a Belamie original.

If Araminta's memory was correct—and it usually was—that clasp matched exactly with the earrings Stella had been wearing. But how could Stella afford Belamie earrings? And why would she have ones that matched a necklace Bertie had already sold?

Stella had been missing from the dining room when Bertie was killed. She'd said she was seeing her relative Daryl Sendquist to the door, but was she really?

Checking the clock, Araminta saw that it was too late to call Daryl now. She thanked the cats and hopped into bed. She couldn't wait for morning to come so she could make that call.

CHAPTER FOURTEEN

The next morning, Araminta dressed early and went out to the garden with her phone. Naturally, the cats followed close behind. The three of them seemed quite interested in her call and sat at her feet, staring up as she punched in Daryl Sendquist's number. Hopefully, his reporter duties required that he rise early, since Araminta had barely been able to wait until eight o'clock to call.

"Mr. Sendquist, this is Araminta Moorecliff."

"Ms. Moorecliff. What a delight! Thank you again for hosting that lovely cat show."

"Meow!" Sasha said from her spot next to Araminta's left foot.

"Umm, yes, well, that is sort of why I am calling."

"Oh?" Daryl sounded intrigued.

"I believe you have an acquaintance that is staying here at Moorecliff Manor. Stella Armentrout."

"Right. Stella. She's actually a second cousin."

Daryl sounded more guarded now. "Is something wrong?"

Araminta's radar pinged. Was he expecting something to be wrong? "Well, there's been a problem. A murder, actually."

Daryl gasped. "Stella was murdered?"

"Goodness, no. Her boss, Bartholomew Belamie."

"Is Stella okay?"

"Yes, she seems fine, but I was wondering... There seems to be some question about her past. The police are still trying to find the murderer and... Well, if I knew what it was, I could perhaps help clear her name." Araminta figured that was the best way to get Daryl to talk.

"Oh, that... It was nothing, really. Stella was totally innocent. That doctor framed her." Daryl's voice rose.

"Doctor?"

"Yes, it happened at Elliott Hospital when she was a nurse." Daryl sighed. "There was some sort of scandal about missing painkillers. She had nothing to do with it, of course, but got blamed anyway. She was fired, and that's why she always loved Mr. Belamie so much. He gave her a job when no one else would."

"I see. That's good to know."

Araminta hung up after half-heartedly assuring Daryl she would do her best to convey Stella's innocence to the police.

She looked down at the three cats, who were all staring up at her expectantly.

"I should have remembered Stella mentioning she

was a nurse… and a nurse would know exactly where to poke someone in the throat in order to kill them."

Before she could slip the phone into her pocket, Ivan called.

"Bad news," Ivan said.

Fear clutched at Araminta's chest. "What happened? Did something happen to Stephanie?"

"No, no nothing like that," Ivan reassured her. "It's about the case. It turns out Stephen Roy has an alibi."

Araminta frowned down at the cats, who were circling her ankles, running toward the house, and then running back again. "You don't say? Are you sure it can be verified?"

"He was in the meeting with Sal the Sledgehammer."

"Who?" Araminta had to admit the criminal element in town certainly had colorful nicknames.

"We nabbed a small-time crook for something else, and he tried to make a deal. Said he was in on this big meeting of the crime bosses. Stephen Roy was one of the ones in attendance, and the meeting was on the night Mr. Belamic was killed, from seven to eight o'clock."

"That's when Bertie was killed, but Stephen was with Viv here at the mansion," Araminta said. "She said she had a headache and was in their room, and he backed her up."

"That's what they said, but maybe Viv was covering for him."

"Or maybe your crook was lying. It doesn't matter,

101

though. I have another good lead." Araminta told him about the pictures and Stella's earrings.

"You think she stole them and killed Bertie?" Ivan asked.

"She might have killed him for another reason and then taken the opportunity to grab the earrings. She does have that sketchy past at the hospital, doesn't she?"

"The pain medicine," Ivan said. "But honestly, I got the impression she was innocent on that one. She said she was framed."

"Well, she was fired, and Bertie didn't like any hint of impropriety in his business. That's why he wouldn't sell the ring to Stephen Roy. What if he really didn't know about her past and then found out that night and they got into an argument and she killed him?"

"It could be." Ivan thought for a few minutes. "But Stella said that Bertie took a chance on her. Wouldn't that imply that he knew about her past?"

"That's what she *said*, but maybe the truth was another matter."

"Okay, I'll see if I can get Bixcombe to bring her in and talk to her again," Ivan said. "Be careful, Araminta. If she's a killer, then talking to her yourself could be dangerous. Maybe you should leave that to the police."

"I'll take that under consideration," Araminta lied. "Well, gotta run!" She hung up the phone and broke into a trot.

ARAMINTA RUSHED INTO THE HOUSE. She had to catch Stella alone somehow before she got away. She ran into Trinity in the back hallway.

"Have you seen Stella this morning?" Araminta asked.

"She's finally come out of her room and is in the dining room. I've put out a buffet. Everyone can serve themselves." Trinity had to yell that last part since Araminta was already racing toward the dining room.

Araminta slowed abruptly as she approached the dining room and entered at a leisurely stroll. "Oh! Good morning, Stella. How delightful to see you've decided to leave your rooms and join us below stairs once again."

At the table, Stella offered a slight smile. "I felt it best I do so and that I leave here soon. I would not wish to overstay my welcome."

"Oh, pooh," Araminta admonished. "You are fine here until you have yourself firmly in order."

She nodded. "Thank you."

Araminta headed to the server that was loaded with silver chafing dishes and surveyed the food as she thought of how best to interrogate Stella. This morning, Mary had provided eggs Benedict, home fries, bacon, and sausage. A fancy Limoges platter with gold trim held a variety of breads, bagels, and Danish. Iced pitchers contained orange juice and tomato juice. Araminta went straight for the coffee carafe then put some eggs on a plate.

Arun, Sasha, and Codger circled as she surveyed the

offerings. "None for you three. Mary has actual cat food for you in the kitchen."

"Have you heard when the coroner will release Bartholomew's body for burial?" Stella asked. "I-I feel I should at least send flowers. I called his sister, but she hasn't called back…"

"Daisy and Ivan are seeing to the arrangements. I am sure she will know more about the details soon."

"And what about the ring cases and Bart's jewelry? The police still have that, and I need to get it back."

Araminta spread her napkin in her lap and then looked up at Stella, deciding that the direct route of questioning was the best. "And why is that? So that you can steal some of it?"

Stella gasped. "What? No! So that I can return it to the store and sell it. As far as I know, I still work for Belamie's. Even though Bart is gone, I assume the store will still go on."

"So did you make it a habit of wearing Belamie jewels?" Araminta asked.

Stella's hands flew to her ears. She was still wearing the pearl-and-diamond earrings. "What? Bertie gifted these to me!"

Araminta gave her a stern look. "That seems odd since they match the necklace that Maisie Perkins bought from him."

"Exactly. Mrs. Perkins wears clip-on earrings, and these are posts." Stella took the earring out of her ear to show Araminta. "So Bertie gifted them to me since they would no longer have a matching necklace."

Araminta wasn't sure what to say. Bertie had been very generous, but... "What about the jewelry tray that was found with the body? You were very vague about whether or not anything was missing."

"That's because I don't know exactly what Bertie had on there. You think I would kill him to steal a pair of earrings?" Stella made a disgusted noise and threw her napkin down on the table. "I can't believe you would think I would steal from that nice man. Why would I do that after he had been so nice to me? And even if I did, why on earth would I wear them right at the dinner table, when he could see them?"

Maybe Araminta shouldn't have rushed to judgement. Had Stella been wearing them that night at the table? Araminta only remembered seeing them after Bertie's death.

"That's right." Stella pushed up then leaned her palms on the table, glaring at Araminta. "He gave them to me before we even came here, and I've been wearing them ever since. And if you want proof, why don't you talk to that crazy photographer lady, Vivianne? She took a picture of me that night in the foyer when I was showing Daryl out. I was wearing these earrings, and I believe at that time, Bertie was very much alive!"

And with that, she flounced out of the room, leaving Araminta feeling like she'd done the very thing Jacob had warned her about—jumping to conclusions before investigating all the clues.

CHAPTER FIFTEEN

*A*raminta's thoughts whirled as she rushed to her room. Was Stella's story about Bertie giving her the earrings true? If not, she might have just tipped off the killer! Even worse, she hadn't gotten the chance to ask Stella about the receipt from Ivan that Stephanie had found on her desk.

She grabbed the camera and plopped down on the bed. The cats jumped up and circled around her before settling in next to her and watching as she scrolled through the pictures.

"Meow!"

"Meeme!"

"Meep!"

Their luminescent eyes slid from hers to the camera as if trying to prod her along. Maybe she should have paid more attention to them before and not been so quick to act on the first picture she saw. She hadn't even looked at everything on the camera before jumping to conclusions about Stella when she saw the necklace on Maisie Perkins.

As she scrolled through again, her eyes were drawn to the timestamps. What time had they been at the dinner table?

Jacob had stopped his watch at 7:23 p.m. Bertie had been stabbed only moments before. Jacob and Bertie had only been gone from the table for a half hour at most. If she could find a picture of Stella wearing the earrings before seven o'clock, it would prove she had worn them in Bertie's presence and thus support her story.

Aha! There it was—a picture of Stella at the front door. It must've been taken right after she'd seen Daryl out. The timestamp was 6:58 p.m., and Stella was wearing the earrings. She'd been telling the truth about Bertie giving them to her.

But wait a minute… What was Viv doing in the foyer at that time?

Vivianne had told the police she'd been in her room with a headache. Stephen Roy had vouched for her. But now, Araminta knew Stephen was at the crime-boss meeting at that time, so he wouldn't have known if Vivianne was in the room.

She scrolled to the next picture. It was of a newel post at the foot of the staircase. It was a cast-iron angel holding a lantern with Tiffany-glass shades. The timestamp was 7:10 p.m.

The next picture was time stamped 7:21 p.m., but it

wasn't really a picture. It was more of a blur of green and brown. *Leaves? Plants?*

Reggie had arrived at 7:19 p.m. and talked to the cabbie for a while. Then he'd stopped to pet Codger, who was coming back to the side door. Reggie had gotten into the mudroom in time to see Jacob put his stopwatch in his pocket at 7:23 p.m.

How had Codger gotten outside? None of the staff had let him out, which meant he probably went out the door after the killer.

Araminta smoothed her hand down his silky fur. "You were chasing the killer, weren't you?"

"Mew." His golden eyes held hers for a few beats, and it felt as if he were telling her he had been.

"Do you know who it is?"

His gaze dropped. "Merroo."

"If only you three could talk." She looked fondly at Arun and Sasha, imagining what it would be like if she could truly communicate with them. "Still, I feel like we can communicate in some ways."

"Mew!"

"Mew mew!"

She turned her attention back to the picture. If Vivianne was the killer and she had fled out the side yard and into the gardens, a hasty picture might have been snapped without her knowing if she fumbled with the camera.

Now things started to make more sense. Stephen hadn't been acting evasive at the Ruemont party when he'd talked to Stephanie and Reggie. When he'd said he'd let Viv take care of it, Armenta had thought he was being vague, but what if he was telling the truth? What if he *had* let Viv take care of everything? It was possible he had no idea how Viv actually got the ring.

She must've arranged to meet with Bertie to buy her ring, but Bertie had refused to sell it to her when he found out she was marrying Stephen Roy. Did Vivianne get so angry that she killed him?

And she knew self-defense, because Trinity had said that Vivianne had threatened a karate move on one of the clerks at the dress fitting, and they'd talked about her self-defense training at the party with Stephanie and Reggie. She'd known where to hit Bertie to cause the damage. Had she stabbed him and taken the ring while he was lying on the floor dying?

But one question remained. Vivianne must have known there were photos on the camera that could prove she was in the foyer shortly before the murder, so why hadn't she noticed the camera was missing?

"Meow!"

Araminta looked down to see three pairs of intelligent cat eyes blinking at her. "You guys were trying to lead me to the clues all along, and I was being too stubborn to follow. I should've known my human bumbling was no match for your feline intelligence. I'd better call Ivan."

CHAPTER SIXTEEN

Araminta waited with Ivan behind the glass of the big two-way mirror at the back of the interrogation room. Inside the other room, Harry Bixcombe dropped a folder on the table in front of the couple who had been awaiting his arrival.

"Mr. Roy. Miss Underwood. Thank you for coming down. I apologize for the room. The other conference rooms are in use at the moment," he said, offering an apologetic smile, the toothpick sticking out of one side of his mouth.

"It's no problem, Detective Bixcombe," Vivianne assured him. "Stephen and I are always happy to accommodate you."

The detective nodded. "Wonderful. Say, do you mind if I show you a few pictures? There are only a few. I promise not to take up too much of your time."

Stephen Roy nodded. "Viv loves pictures. She's into photography, as you might like to know."

Again, Bixcombe nodded. Then he reached inside the folder and pulled out a photo. "Do you recognize this place?"

Vivianne leaned over Stephen to see the photograph then leaned back again, her expression gleeful. "Oh, yes! That's the Ruemont place. We were there a few days ago, remember, Stephen? For the big gala event?"

Stephen glanced at Bixcombe, who arched a brow in question. He nodded.

"I see," the detective said. "Well, then, how about this one? And this one?"

More pictures of the Ruemont event were shown.

"Yes, those are all from the event," Vivianne said.

"Viv's cameras were all destroyed. Good thing you uploaded these pictures first," Stephen said.

Vivianne frowned.

"Destroyed?" Bixcombe leaned forward, one brow raised.

"Freak accident," Stephen said. "She kept them all in a rolling suitcase, and it fell in the pool! Viv had taken it out there to sort through the pictures after we got home."

"It was a tragedy," Vivianne said.

"I see." Bixcombe leaned back in his chair, his gaze fixed on Vivianne. "Miss Vivianne, I hear you're quite good at karate."

She shifted in her seat. "Well, I don't know if I'd say I'm quite good…"

"She is," Stephen said proudly. "I had her taught by

the best. A woman can never be too careful when it comes to self-defense."

"Defense classes, maybe? From this man?" The detective pulled another picture from the folder.

Again, Vivianne nodded. "Shapiro. Aldean Shapiro." She leaned forward, her expression serious. "He's extremely thorough. I learned a lot."

"I'm sure you did." Bixcombe leaned forward again. "Well, it seems I only have a couple more photographs here, if you're sure you don't mind?"

Vivianne waved her left hand toward the table and smiled when the light caught the cut of her diamond. "Go ahead. Let's see what you have."

The first picture hit the table. It was a photo of the angel newel post.

Viv frowned. "That would be a shot from the interior of Moorecliff Manor."

Bixcombe nodded, and then a second one—the last photo in the detective's folder—hit the table. Vivianne's smile disappeared. It was the photo of the blurry leaves, the timestamp circled in red.

Vivianne's frowned deepened. "What's that? I don't understand..." But her expression said she did understand.

"That's the side garden at Moorecliff Manor. See the timestamp? That's only a few seconds after Mr. Belamie was stabbed."

She glanced at Stephen, who looked perplexed. Her expression said she knew where all this was going, but that it was far too late to do anything about what was coming.

"Well, this picture doesn't prove anything, and you can't even prove I took it," Vivianne said.

"We have the camera with your fingerprints."

"The camera? But they all fell in the pool..." Stephen looked at Vivianne uncertainly. "By accident, right?"

"Of course." Vivianne managed to look insulted.

Bixcombe shifted the toothpick to the other side of his mouth. "So you say, but there is other evidence against you, and it all adds up. Vivianne Underwood, you are under arrest for the murder of Bartholomew Belamie," the detective said as he stood and came around the table to put cuffs on her wrists.

Stephen looked shocked. "Hey wait a minute. You can't arrest her. She's my fiancée! Viv, tell them it's not true."

Vivianne couldn't look Stephen in the eye. "I... I can't lie to you."

"But why?" Stephen asked.

She sniffed. "I just wanted a Belamie ring."

"But you said you got the ring you wanted." Stephen looked confused.

"I got it, but I didn't *buy* it. That jerk Belamie wouldn't sell it to us. Didn't want to tarnish his precious business reputation. So I got angry, and things went too far." Viv looked down at the floor, tears spilling from her eyes. "I didn't mean to kill him. All I wanted was the ring. Don't you see?"

114

Behind the glass, the sound shut off, and Ivan's breath left him in a woosh of relief.

Araminta smiled. "We knew all along that Jacob couldn't have done it, Ivan, and now you have proof."

His smile was shaky. "Araminta Moorecliff, I don't know how you came up with that camera, but I am forever grateful you did… and I hope you will excuse me later for my forwardness, but I am going to hug you now, whether you like it or not."

And so he did. And she hugged him back, because she did not mind in the least.

But there was one last mystery that Araminta hadn't solved. What was the receipt with the Hershey name on it that Stella had in her room for?

CHAPTER SEVENTEEN

*A*fter Vivianne had been taken care of, Detective Bixcombe came to the conference room to let Araminta and Ivan know the order had been sent through for Jacob's release.

"I guess Viv didn't realize she had left that camera behind at the manor," Araminta said.

Bixcombe shook his head. "She assumed it was inside the case that fell in the pool and was tossed out with the others. Of course the whole pool incident was on purpose. She confessed just a few seconds ago that she was worried there might be something incriminating on one of the cameras and figured the best way to ruin them was to get them wet."

"Lucky for us she was a bit disorganized and scattered. Otherwise, she would have noticed it was missing, and we wouldn't have seen those pictures," Araminta said.

"Right. Well, it looks like you've come through for

us once again, Ms. Moorecliff." Bixcombe's sincere compliment surprised Araminta. He held out his hand for hers and shook it. "You have the full gratitude of myself and my team."

"*My* team," Ivan corrected. He grinned and clapped the detective on the back. "You are welcome to the credit for this one, Bix. Thanks to you, my grandfather can come home again, and for that, I am grateful."

Bixcombe smiled. "It seems I may have misjudged you, Hershey. I assumed your tenure here on the force was because your grandfather pulled strings, but judging by what I've seen you doing behind the scenes, that may not be the case. But the truth is, the credit belongs to Araminta. Without her foresight and creative thinking, we may never have caught Vivianne, and your grandfather might still be behind bars."

"Never," came a gruff, familiar voice from the doorway. Araminta, Ivan, and Bixcombe all turned to see Jacob in the waiting area outside the conference room. He pointed to Araminta. "This lady could run circles around the three of us and not even break a sweat when it comes to figuring out who did it, gentlemen. With her on the case, there was never any doubt in my mind whether or not I'd be free."

"Not even for a second, Grandfather?" Ivan teased.

Jacob shook his head. "Not one. If there had been, do you think I would have bothered to go to the trouble of arranging a meeting at Moorecliff Manor in the middle of a cat show to get these from Bartholomew?"

He held up a glittering set of rings. "Stella was nice enough to bring those by right as I got out."

Araminta was confused. "You bought rings from Bertie? What did you need those for, Jacob?"

"Because I couldn't ask you to marry me without a ring for your lovely finger, now could I?" He looked at Ivan. "Not sure that's the best way to do it, son, but at least I've done it now."

Ivan blinked then tossed back his head and laughed. "It's as good a way as any, Grandfather. I, myself, recently did the same but over a headset in the middle of an undercover sting operation."

Detective Bixcombe shook his head at the trio. "I'm not sure if I've followed everything that just happened here, but you Hersheys certainly go from murder investigations to weddings rather quickly."

Araminta arched a brow. "Well, I haven't said yes yet."

Silence filled the room.

For an instant, uncertainty flickered in Jacob's eyes. He went to her then and took her hands in his. "Araminta, dearest, love. Joy of my life. Will you do me the honor of welcoming me into your life wholeheartedly?"

She tilted her head and peered up at him. "Better, but that's still the wrong question, I think."

Jacob sighed. His shoulders rose and fell with a silent chuckle. "Minta, will you marry me?"

Araminta smiled. "Yes. This time, my answer is yes, as it should have been years ago and now forever will be."

THERE WAS a big celebration at Moorecliff Manor that night. Trays of appetizers were set out on the credenza in the front parlor, while everyone drank champagne from the family's best crystal flutes.

Harold, Trinity, Mary, and the staff were forbidden from serving and showed up in their finest to mingle with the Moorecliffs as part of the family. Everyone was excited at the prospect of a wedding… or two… at Moorecliff Manor.

"Two weddings? Yech!" Codger settled in the corner away from the trampling feet of the partygoers.

Arun sighed. "I suppose that will mean more crowds of people descending on us."

"It's just a minor inconvenience. Don't you want Araminta to be happy?" Sasha's sapphire eyes glittered under the light of the chandelier.

"I suppose. I'll just look forward to when they are all gone and we can go back to our usual routine with Araminta." Arun eyed a silver tray of crab puffs that sat on one of the side tables. If he hopped up on the chair, he could just about reach it.

"Wait a minute." Codger interrupted his preening routine and looked up at them. "Won't Araminta want to live with Jacob and me?"

"Of course they'll live together, but that will be here at Moorecliff Manor. It's her ancestral home." Sasha was sure of it.

"But… but… I was thinking Jacob and I could

return to our small cottage bachelor pad." Codger seemed quite distraught.

"Sorry," Arun kept his eye on the crab puffs. "I don't think that's going to happen."

Codger's eyes slitted as he glared through the crowd at Jacob. He kept silent, but Arun could see he was truly upset. He felt bad for him, but he was glad Araminta—and therefore he and Sasha—would stay here, even if it did mean that Jacob and Codger would be added to the mix.

"I can't believe Araminta suspected Stella after she so nicely kept Jacob's surprise a secret!" Sasha said.

"There were several clues that pointed toward her," Arun reminded her.

"I suppose, but at least Araminta was surprised in the end."

"And Jacob's name was cleared," Codger added.

The chocolate fur on Sasha's forehead wrinkled. "I do worry about the wedding, though. All those people traipsing about... Someone might end up dead."

"Bah! We've had enough of bodies and secrets, don't you think?" Arun glanced at Sasha, who looked away.

"I suppose. Enough about that. Did you guys see that tray of salmon pâtè over by the fireplace? I say we trot over and see if we can get Harold to slip us a few bites." Sasha stretched and headed toward the tray.

Arun exchanged a glance with Codger. Was it his imagination, or was Sasha acting a little strange?

Codger shrugged and fluffed out his tail. "I think

she has a good idea. Let's go. We deserve a reward for a job well done, don't you think?"

Arun couldn't argue with that. As he followed behind Codger and Sasha, a feeling of contentment settled over him. They'd solved another murder and cleared Jacob's name, and both humans and cats were happily celebrating. Things were going well; hopefully, they would stay that way for a long time.

****

Sign up for my newsletter and get my latest releases at the lowest discount price, plus I'll send you a link for a free download of a book in one of my other series:

https://leighanndobbscozymysteries.gr8.com

If you want to receive a text message on your cell phone when I have a new release, text COZYMYSTERY to (603) 709-2906 (sorry, this only works for US cell phones!)

Join my readers group on Facebook:
https://www.facebook.com/groups/ldobbsreaders

Like my Facebook Author Page:
https://www.facebook.com/leighanndobbsbooks

MORE BOOKS BY LEIGHANN DOBBS:

Cozy Mysteries

Mystic Notch
Cat Cozy Mystery Series
* * *

Ghostly Paws
A Spirited Tail
A Mew To A Kill
Paws and Effect
Probable Paws
A Whisker of a Doubt
Wrong Side of the Claw
Claw and Order

Oyster Cove Guesthouse
Cat Cozy Mystery Series
***

124

Buried Secrets
Deadly Intentions
A Grave Mistake
Spell Found
Fatal Fortune
Hidden Secrets

Kate Diamond Mystery Adventures
***

Hidden Agemda (Book 1)
Ancient Hiss Story (Book 2)
Heist Society (Book 3)

Mooseamuck Island
Cozy Mystery Series
* * *

A Zen For Murder
A Crabby Killer
A Treacherous Treasure

Lexy Baker
Cozy Mystery Series
* * *

Lexy Baker Cozy Mystery Series Boxed Set Vol 1 (Books 1-4)

Or buy the books separately:

125

Killer Cupcakes
Dying For Danish
Murder, Money and Marzipan
3 Bodies and a Biscotti
Brownies, Bodies & Bad Guys
Bake, Battle & Roll
Wedded Blintz
Scones, Skulls & Scams
Ice Cream Murder
Mummified Meringues
Brutal Brulee (Novella)
No Scone Unturned
Cream Puff Killer
Never Say Pie

Lady Katherine Regency Mysteries
***

An Invitation to Murder (Book 1)
The Baffling Burglaries of Bath (Book 2)
Murder at the Ice Ball (Book 3)
A Murderous Affair (Book 4)
Murder on Charles Street (Book 5)

Hazel Martin Historical Mystery Series
***

Murder at Lowry House (book 1)
Murder by Misunderstanding (book 2)

Sam Mason Mysteries
(As L. A. Dobbs)
***

Telling Lies (Book 1)
Keeping Secrets (Book 2)
Exposing Truths (Book 3)
Betraying Trust (Book 4)
Killing Dreams (Book 5)

Romantic Comedy
***
Corporate Chaos Series

In Over Her Head (book 1)
Can't Stand the Heat (book 2)
What Goes Around Comes Around (book 3)
Careful What You Wish For (4)

Contemporary Romance
***
Reluctant Romance

Sweet Romance (Written As Annie Dobbs)
Firefly Inn Series

***

Another Chance (Book 1)
Another Wish (Book 2)

Hometown Hearts Series
***
No Getting Over You (Book 1)
A Change of Heart (Book 2)

Sweet Mountain Billionaires
***

Jaded Billionaire (Book 1)
A Billion Reasons Not To Fall In Love (Book 2)

Regency Romance
* * *

Scandals and Spies Series:
Kissing The Enemy
Deceiving the Duke
Tempting the Rival
Charming the Spy
Pursuing the Traitor
Captivating the Captain

ABOUT THE AUTHOR

USA Today best-selling Author, Leighann Dobbs, has had a passion for reading since she was old enough to hold a book, but she didn't put pen to paper until much later in life. After a twenty-year career as a software engineer, with a few side trips into selling antiques and making jewelry, she realized you can't make a living reading books, so she tried her hand at writing them and discovered she had a passion for that, too! She lives in New Hampshire with her husband, Bruce, their trusty Chihuahua mix, Mojo, and beautiful rescue cat, Kitty.

Find out about her latest books by signing up at:
    https://leighanndobbscozymysteries.gr8.com

If you want to receive a text message alert on your cell phone for new releases , text COZYMYSTERY to (603) 709-2906 (sorry, this only works for US cell phones!)

Connect with Leighann on Facebook
    http://facebook.com/leighanndobbsbooks

Made in the USA
Monee, IL
28 May 2022

97172516R00075